The Right Place by C. E. Montague

A Book of Pleasures

Charles Edward Montague was born in London on New Year's Day, 1867 and educated at the City of London School and then Balliol College, Oxford.

At university, Montague, a keen writer, wrote several literary reviews for the Manchester Guardian and was then invited for a month's trial and, after impressing, to work there.

Montague and the editor, C. P. Scott shared the same political views and between them they turned the Manchester Guardian into a vibrant and campaigning newspaper. They were for Irish Home Rule and against the Boer War and the First World War.

But now that the war had begun. Montague believed that it was important to give full and unequivocal support to the British government. Despite his age, 47, he was determined to serve.

Montague was soon promoted to the rank of second lieutenant and with it a transfer to Military Intelligence. The war also brought about a crisis in his faith and it was resolved by Montague temporarily putting it to one side and carrying on with the fighting.

In November 1918 the war was over and Montague could now return home to his wife and family and also to the Manchester Guardian where he would continue to work until retirement in 1925.

For Montague the war had been corrosive but it had given him much to write about both for the paper but also for his books which he now hoped to also spend more time on. Among those to flow from his pen are the novels A Hind Let Loose and Rough Justice as well as collections of short stories, other essays and a travel book.

He finally retired in 1925, and settled down to become a full-time writer in the last years of his life. Charles Edward Montague died in Manchester on May 28th, 1928 at the age of 61.

Index of Contents

CHAPTER I

OVERTURE

Sun, and sky, and breeze, and solitary walks, and summer holidays, and the greenness of fields, and the delicious juices of meats and fishes, and society, and the cheerful glass, and candle-light, and fireside conversations, and innocent vanities, and jests, and irony itself—do these things go out with life?
LAMB.

I

You may wonder how it will feel, to find you are old, and able to travel no more. Perhaps to sit out, with your legs up, in an invalid chair on a lawn when the warm weather comes, and to finger a book of time-tables for trains, and to think how at this hour the day express from Paris is probably nearing Mulhouse and the evening freshness of air that has blown across snow is coming in at the windows; soon the train will be slowing to clank into the station at Bale just when the first lamps are lit in the town and look gay in the twilight. How the Rhine must be swishing along, aplashing, glimmering coolness heard more than seen, below the balconied windows of rooms at the Three Kings Hotel, where the blest, who have just come from England, are giving a sigh of content as they throw their dusty gloves down on a bed.

Perhaps to lie awake, as the old do, through English August dawns, remembering many past awakenings in trains when day was breaking over Delemont or Porrentruy, and houses half seen through the blenching windows seemed to have taken wide eaves upon themselves during the night; brooks, silent all across France, had begun to make little jovial noises, and clouds had come down from the sky to tumble about on the fields. To live with dim ghosts—quite kindly ghosts, but dim—of the warm blooded hours of old autumn journeys to Italy, up to meet the bleaching chill that creeps in October from Goeschenen down to Lucerne; and then the plunge into the tunnel's murmurous darkness under the very hub, the middle boss of all Europe, the rocky knot in which all her stone sinews are tied at their ends into one central bunch; and then the emergence, translating you out of a Teuton into a Latin world, from grizzled wintry tonelessness to burnished lustre, all the lingering opulence of sun-fed brown and yellow, purple and crimson and rose—Airolo, Bellinzona, Lugano, all aglow and deep-hearted, like rubies or wine, in that Giorgionian champaign of olive and mulberry.

The blasphemies that have been written and talked! I do not mean so much the irreligious rubbish about a Hell after this life. Man, as a whole, has learnt reverence enough to withdraw that grossest of all the slurs which he put, in his moody, ignorant youth, on the goodness of God. Much of his talk about Heaven itself has been sacrilegious enough. When the Claudio of Measure for Measure, the poor little gluttonous sheep that had fatted himself for the butcher, was wriggling and swerving away from the knife, his bleating was all about positive post-mortem pains that he had heard tell of. Burning and freezing were much on his mind, and blowing about, round the world, in the grip of high winds, and rotting without anaesthetics. He knew by heart the pick of all the cruel freaks that men made after the image of beasts used to impute to a god that they had made after the image of themselves. But if the terrified weakling had had any brains he might have been almost as deeply disturbed by a review of the set of sensations commonly advertised in his time as amenities laid up in Heaven to crown the just and the forgiven.

Some of these subtler terrors of death survive in a few unfortunate minds to this day. The last has yet to be heard of the flavourless heaven of tireless limbs and sexless souls, tearless eyes and choirs of effortless and infallible intonation. Imagine eternal youth with no impulse to walk in the ways of its heart, and in the sight of its eyes, and deposed for ever from its august and precarious stewardship of the clean blood of a race! Conceive the light that never was on sea or land, no longer caught in broken gleams through visionary forests, but blazing away like the lamps on common lodging-house stairs; and the peace that passeth all understanding explored and explained, to the last letter, inside and out! Think, if you can bear to do it, what your existence would be without wonder, or any need for valiant hope, or for resolution unassisted by hope, a life no longer salt with savoursome vicissitudes; all the hardy, astringent conditions of joy, and the purchase-money of rapture, abolished for ever. No, better not think of it. "It is too horrible."

Life must have been pretty hard in some of the ages, that any prospect so dreadful should have illuded people's minds as a compensation or a deliverance. Perhaps if one's body were chained for life to an oar in a galley, or sold into some darksome underground slavery, like a pit pony, one might, without positive meanness or impudence, put in a claim upon God for some portion of pleasure and ease hereafter in lieu of all that one had missed. But you and I—!

We that grew up by the Thames among roses and apples, and walked home from school of an evening down the nave of St. Paul's and through the courts of the Temple, and heard the chimes from Oxford towers at midnight and lived elately in the rhythms of her jocund choruses and racing oars! We that have failed and thriven and been rich and poor, on our little scale, and have been happy in our love and found work after our hearts and rambled in sun and mist over Pennine and Cumbrian hills and seen sunset and dawn from great peaks of the Alps and across several seas and over lost battles and victories—what sort of peasant slaves should we be to come full from the feast with a whine for victuals more savoury? Away to Mrs. Gamp, wheresoever she be, with talk of vales of tears, and life's dull round, and stony places of pilgrimage. There is no hiding it—we like the stones, and always did, and the round has been a merry-go-round, and against the whole vale there is not one serious word to be said. Perhaps a proper canniness, a sound business instinct, ought to keep men and women from owning how good a time they have had since they were set down on the earth. Early man dealt pretty shrewdly with his gods; he drove hard bargains with them; he even starved or beat them when they had not done as well as they might. And some traces of this prudent instinct are still astir in mankind. Careful souls seem still to whisper to themselves that there may be much to come yet; the great "deal" has only begun; were it not rash to let out how pleased and astonished you are with the terms you have hitherto got? For if you do that in a market, the other party sees daylight at once; he thinks what a fool he has been to offer so much, when less would have done: and so he stiffens his terms. And no doubt there is some very respectable warrant for viewing your soul's relations with God as strict business matters.

Whatever, Lord, we lend to Thee
Repaid a thousandfold will be;
Then gladly will we give to Thee.

It sounds like good sense. And yet a sneaking doubt will creep in. We cannot feel so sure about that dour driver of bargains, against whom we are advised to take these sagacious precautions. Another God we can conceive; but not, with any vividness, a God with whom you have to be careful lest He see what a soft thing He has given you. And then there is another doubt. Haggle we never so wisely, is there any tremendous coup left for our arts to bring off? Heaven is here already; no flaming swords keep from the gate the man that knows how to value the garden. "I am in love with this green earth; the face of town and country; the unspeakable rural solitudes and the sweet security of streets. I would set up my tabernacle here." Of what avail to bargain further, when you have got all? Why not give yourself away, as that heaven gives itself, and recklessly confess the amenity of your condition ever since you first shivered and grinned with a small boy's delight in the feel of a pavement through the thin rubber soles of your shoes, and snuffed up queer and engaging fumes of romance with the mixed smell of engines and fog under the resonant roof of Waterloo station?

So, at least, it befits me to plead, having to make, in the pages that follow, some undiplomatic admissions of full satisfaction with certain contents of life on the earth. The only misgiving about them which strikes me now as worth entertaining is Solomon's, lest the grinders should cease because they are few, and those that look out of the window be darkened. So here goes, before the panes have time to be fogged, or a grasshopper, such as the work of writing a little book, to become a burden.

CHAPTER II

HOLIDAYS

Holidays—the only kind of cake that makes bread eat better after it.
ANON

I

Children are often too tired to sleep, and the worst thing about overwork is the way it may make you unfit for a holiday. You may be left able only to stand still and blink, like used-up horses when put out to grass, while the man who has worked in reason, and worried no more than he should, is off for the day or the month, to plunge into some kind of work not his own, just for the fun of the thing.

For all the best sport is the doing, for once, of somebody else's work. The wise cashier puts in a spell of steady exertion as a gardener. Statesmen, prelates and judges of appeal come as near as they can to fulfilling the functions of good professional golfers, fishermen or chauffeurs. The master minds who run our railways for us may seem to flee the very sight of a permanent way; but they don rucksacks for ten-hour tramps over rock, peat and bracken, such as the lighter kind of porters used to take for their living in the days before steam. The new-made husband and head of a house, released from his desk in a public office, will labour absorbedly from morning until dewy eve to put the attic in order or get the whole of the tool-shed painted while yet it is light, proud and happy as Pepys when after a day of such application he put the glorious result down in his diary, adding—lest pride should grow sinful—"Pray God my mind run not too much upon it."

Is it, then, mere change of work that makes the best holiday? Scarcely. The master cotton-spinner would not find it sport to spend his August in ruling a dye-works. There is no rush of Civil Service clerks for a month's diversion, each year, among the ledgers of joint-stock banks in the City. A doubtful legend, as we all know, reports that if ever one of the old London drivers of horsed 'buses had a holiday—and even this is uncertain—he spent it in driving his wife and himself out into the country in a small trap. Suppose it was true. Yet even then, mark you, a small trap of the period had only one horse. And that leads to the point. What most charms us as play is not merely some other kind of work than our own. It is some kind more elementary.

Not that we want to bestow on this holiday work anything less than the whole of our energy. On our Bank Holidays do not we bend up every corporal agent to the sport? We sweat in the eye of Phoebus; we take it out of ourselves, yea, all of it. Just what we want, in our hearts, is to put forth our powers, for once in a while, upon some occupation in which our endeavour shall go, or at least seem to go, a mighty long way, and not go it in some direction which we have never intended. Most of our working time is spent in making for some distant objective—fame, or the good of our kind, or a golden wall or spire, or some other estimable thing. But the line of approach to these goals is not very clear, and then there is always the plaguy chance that, if ever we get there, the gold may turn out to be gilt. If we be parsons, Heaven knows when we shall have the parish reasonably sober. If we be doctors, perhaps casting out one bacterial devil by letting another loose at it, how can we feel secure against making some deadly slip in the dark, like the man who let the first rabbit loose in Australia? In any kind of responsible work, be it only the work of rearing a family decently well, the way is dark and we are far from home. That is the real curse of Adam; not the work in itself but the worry and doubt of ever getting it done; perhaps the doubt, also, whether, after all, it ought to be done, or done at the price. All your working year you chase some phantom moment at which you might fairly say "Now I am there." Then Easter comes; you sail your own boat through a night of dirty weather from the Mersey to the Isle of Man; and, as you lower sail in Douglas harbour, you are there; no phantom this time; the curse of Adam is taken clean off you, at any rate for that morning. Or those seeds that you sowed in the back garden on that thrilling Saturday evening amaze and exalt you by coming up, and you learn in your proper person what the joys of discovery and creation are; you have, so far, succeeded in life and done what it piqued you to do in this world. All play, of course, and the victory tiny. Still, on its own scale and for its miniature lifetime, the little model is perfect; the humble muddler has come nearer than anything else is likely to bring him to feeling what the big triumphs of human power must taste like.

II

Man's job on the earth seems to be always becoming more intricate and advanced. Quite early he has to plunge on and on into deepening forests of complexity as his youth penetrates with uncertain feet the central wilds and dark places of algebra-books. The toughness of our task, as compared with that of a hen, is said to be roughly indicated by the contrast between the preparation required for each; the hen is fairly ripe for its labours the day it is born; a man is by no means always efficient after he has afforded employment to a cohort of nurses, governesses, schoolmasters, tutors and professors for more than a score of years. And so, as we proceed with this obscure and intractable undertaking, we dearly like, on our days off, to turn back and do over again, for the fun and easiness of the thing, what we or others really had to do, for dear life, in the infancy of the race.

When Easter releases the child, in any provincial suburb, from his inveterate bondage to grammar and sums, you will see him refreshing himself with sportive revivals of one of the earliest anxieties of man. Foraging round like a magpie or rook, he collects odd bits of castaway tarpaulin and sacking, dusters, old petticoats, broken broom-sticks and fragments of corrugated iron. Assembling these building materials on some practicable patch of waste grass, preferably in the neighbourhood of water, he raises for himself a simple dwelling. The blessing of a small fire crowns these provisions for domestic felicity, and marvellous numbers of small persons may be seen sitting round these rude hearths, conversing with the gravity of Sioux chieftains or, at a menace of rain, packing themselves into incredibly small cubic spaces of wigwam.

Houses, of course, have been somewhat scarce in late years. Parents, no doubt, have shaken their heads over the dearth, and this may have reinforced in their young the primitive human craving to start by getting a roof over one's head. The war, too, with all its talk of tent and hut, dug-out and bivouac, may have fortified the old impulse. Still, it is there, always and anyhow. It is the holiday impulse of self-rescue from that strange and desolating blindness which comes of knowing things too well and taking them as matters of course. Most of us have long become so used to the idea of living in a house that the idea has lost its old fascination. Of course we do value a house, in a way. That is, we are sorely put out if we cannot obtain one. And, having obtained it, we feel deeply wronged if we have forgotten the latch-key some night and cannot get in. But sheer delight in the very notion of a house, the chuckling, thigh-slapping triumph of early man when first he built one—this has died down in us, just as has the grinning and capering glee of the same pioneer when he got the first fire to kindle.

In the orally transmitted Scriptures of some of the Australian blacks the Creator, Pund-jel, was so well pleased when he had fashioned the first man out of clay and bark that he danced for joy round this admirable piece of handiwork. Even the more staid Jehovah of our own Book of Genesis went on from finding his earlier products "good" to find the whole week's work "very good," the exultant complacency of the artist increasing, as it always does, *pari passu* with the activity of his invention. Man has been proceeding, ever since, with the work that was thus started. A house, a bed, a wheel, a boat, a plough— rapturously must his mind have capered, like Pund-jel's, round each of these happy masterpieces when it was new. So, too, would it caper now, but for some pestilent bar that familiarity interposes between us and the deft miracles of gumption that make us able to sit and look out, dry and warm, half an inch from a tempest of snow, and lie ensconced in tiny cubes of snug stillness hoisted up as high as the top of a tree amidst the raving and whining of violent winter winds.

In poets, perhaps, and in a few other people doubly charged with relish for all the contents of existence, some traces of that jubilation persist. Any child who is happily placed and wisely reared has his chance of reviving it for himself. There come to him exultant ecstasies of climbing in trees with the zest of the first tree-dweller in his ancient pedigree; he huddles in holes that he has digged for himself with all the gusto and pride of a pioneer caveman; then from the joys of the domestic cave he passes on to the sweets of the original ramshackle tent, symbol of the opening of the nomad stage in the life of his kind. Packed as miraculously tight into his own small life as a hyacinth, flower and leaves and all, is compressed in the bulb, there unfolds itself for his diversion a stirring recapitulation of the adventurous life of mankind on the earth: he re-lives with relish the whole career of his race; he has been with other ape-like figures in the upper boughs of trees and has shivered with delicious apprehension in caverns of the earth, undergoing a sort of painless return of the terrors of naked savages crouched in imperfect cover, with roaring beasts ranging the forests without. No wonder the little ragged boys are both happy and grave as they sit in pow-wow at the door of a tabernacle composed of two aged sacks, or lean upon their one-foot-high stockade of bits of turf and scan the enigmatic horizon.

III

All fortunate holiday travel, like all good recovery after illness, is a renewal of youth. All the rest of the year your youth is running down within you. The salt of living—not of success and arrival but of mere living, the conscious adventure—is losing its savour; insensibly the days are coming near "when thou shalt say, I have no pleasure in them." We may be toiling or fussing away in the van of some sort of big human march. And quite right too of course; marches have to go on; there is no dropping out of the column; on active service you cannot resign. And yet it may grow hard to keep your zest for the simpler, ruder, basic good things of existence while fingering some of its latest subtleties. What fun the alphabet was, once! But you almost forget, in your present wrestlings with words of six syllables. The rooms where you work are so well heated, without any effort of yours, that willy-nilly you come to forget what the joy of repelling cold is; you may have to sit for so much of the day that the rapture of rest after real fatigue of the body becomes merely words, a thing in a book, not an object of sense; streets and trains and cars are rendered, by some impersonal forces unknown, so utterly safe that safety becomes a mere matter of course, with no power to rouse or astonish; meals appear with an unfailing air of automatism, so that the start of delight with which, in another state of yourself, you look upon a laid dinner-table, with all its centuries of accumulations of 'cute dodges for refining the use of pasture, does not visit you now; even that divine and yet most human contrivance, a bed, the ultimate product of tens of thousands of years of man's nightly consideration of means for being still snugger next night, may lose its power of making you chuckle as you plunge in between the sheets.

But then come holidays. They soon put things to rights. In his story of Marius, Walter Pater describes his hero's recovery of a lost interest in common things—household customs, the daily meals, just the eating of ordinary food at appointed and recurrent times: Marius awoke to regained enjoyment of "that poetic and, as it were, moral significance which surely belongs to all the means of daily life, could we but break through the veil of our familiarity with things by no means vulgar in themselves." Some such retransfiguration of things that had sunk into triteness blesses the fortunate holidaymaker. The sandwiches eaten with grimy fingers at the top of the Napes on Great Gable attain a strange quality of pleasantness; the meal, like every meal that has not somehow gone wrong, achieves a touch of sacramental significance; and the subsequent smoke is the true pipe of peace once more, redolent of spiritual harmonies and romantic dreams. Bodily safety, a treasure charmless to the mind in ordinary life, regains the piquant value of a thing that will not just come of itself; it has to be wooed; the winning of it depends on the right exertion of some faculty not too perplexing to be joyous—the yachtsman's handling of his craft, the climber's hold on rock, the swimmer's sureness of himself across half a mile of deep water. Best of all when the security of every one in a party depends upon the alertness and fitness of each of the others. Then you revivify all human comradeship too; it comes back cleared of the blur that may have dulled your sense of it at home, where human interdependence may be so intricate and so incessant and often so muddled up with annoying circumstances that it seems more tiresome than real, like a virtue vulgarised by the stale eulogistic phrasing of rhetoricians.

In such a sport as mountaineering, vicissitudes of heat and cold are again, for a few make-believe hours, the hazards that they must have been to the houseless man of the prime; sunset and dawn are recharged with the freshness and wonder that they might have had on the morning and the evening of the first day. Rightly to perceive a thing, in all the fullness of its qualities, is really to create it. So, on perfect holidays, you re-create your world and sign on again as a pleased and enthusiastic member of the great air-ship's company. The word recreation seems to tell you as much, and I suppose the old poets hinted it too in their tale of Antaeus, whose strength would all come back with a rush whenever he got a good kiss of his mother the earth.

IV

Something in modern ways of work seems to make some little nip of artificial excitement, of one sort or another, an object of sharper desire than it was. Labour in great mills and workshops and large counting-houses is probably healthier now, for the body, than ever before. Yet there seems to have been some loss for the mind and the spirits. Perhaps it comes of a cause that cannot be helped any more than an army can help the defects of a landscape through which it must pass in the course of a long march. The cause, I suppose, is the inevitable minute subdivision of labour. To put it roughly, the old-time workman made a thing; the modern workman only gives a passing touch to a thing while it is being made. Forty years ago a small Thames boat-builder, working alone in his shed, would make a whole boat, of a very beautiful build, by himself, from its keel to the last lick of its varnish. He got his share—and you could see him get it if you were friends with him—of that joy and excitement of creation in which healthy children at play are at one with inventors and discoverers. The passing of the greater part of that happy excitement away from so many modern modes of manufacture has been a real Fall of Man. It has gone some way to make work what it is said to have been to Adam after his misfortune—a thing to be got through and borne with, because you cannot go on living upon any other terms.

The thing has gone so far that at any trade-union meeting to-day you would not expect to hear a word implying that the work its members do is anything but a mere cause of weariness, only made endurable by pay; this although all work which has not somehow gone wrong is like the work of a normal artist—a thing for which the artist means to get properly paid if he can, but also a thing which he would go on doing anyhow, whether any one paid him or not. You will see men fairly rushing away from the factory gate to get a little excitement out of a bet or a League match. Many of them, and some of the best, may be unconsciously looking for something to put in the place of that satisfying stir of heart and mind which visits every good craftsman during his exhilarating struggle with a testing piece of work. Their work has failed to yield it. They hunt for substitutes for the lost joys of their trade, and of all substitutes an active holiday is the best. The finer or longer holiday a man or woman can get whose work is an eternal picking-up of pins or dipping of match-heads in phosphorus, the greater their chance of remaining decently human. Some inarticulate sense of this may be showing itself in the almost frenzied grasp which new millions are making now at every possible holiday—not in laziness but in a sane instinctive effort to keep the salt of their existence from losing its savour.

V

One special kind of holiday deserves a note to itself. The military experience of the nation went to show that one of the best days of a leave, during the war, was the day before you went. And then it sometimes happened, for reasons of State, that you did not go, after all. Still, you had had your hour. Pro tem., at any rate, you had divinely lived. To put it at the lowest, you had, like the three famous sportsmen of song, powler't up and down a bit and had a rattling day with the home railway time-tables, tasting, as you looked up train by train, the delights of passing the hedged closes of tasselled hops in Kent or the blue bloom of the moors about your home in Yorkshire. Well, if that was better than nothing, why not go in for such fragments of joy, on a system?

The plan is to say to yourself in a firm tone that on such or such a date you are going to some longed-for place; then to make all the fond mental preparations of good travellers, tracking every mile on the map, forming conjectural visions of what you would see from this point and from that; and then, at the last moment, not to go at all, being quite unable to afford it, as you had always known. One solid merit in this sort of travel is that the fares cannot be raised against you, as has so often and so lamentably been done to the impoverishment or immobilisation of those who travel in the flesh. Another advantage is that it overcomes the difficulty which so many of us find in leaving our work for more than a month, perhaps even a fortnight, at a time. From the journey over the Andes, for instance, from the Argentine to the Chilean coast, most of us are inexorably barred by iron laws of time, space and finance. Yet is it evidently a delectable passage; and by a proper use of South American time-tables you can adjust consummately the timing of your transit across the spacious place of origin of bully beef to the iced spike of Aconcagua or the snowy dome of Chimborazo; freely you choose the hour at which it will give you the most exquisite vibrations to stare for the first time at the Pacific; sagaciously you distribute your time between the Arctic, the sub-Arctic, the temperate, the sub-tropical and the tropical zones of the rapid western slope, right down from the high ice to the palms and the warm surf. Much valuable time, again, may doubtless be saved, when visiting New Zealand and crossing her Alps from the side which streams with glaciers to the side tangled with almost tropical jungle, if you have disengaged yourself in time from the conventional impression that your mere bodily presence is required. And yet, yet—I fear I am a carnal man; the homeliest meal of new places seen with the vulgar bodily eye—a mere dish of herbs—allures me more than the lordliest of Barmecide banquets, even the stalled oxen of fancy. And yet, again, there may be something in it if all actual travel, the positive transport of the rejoicing tenement of clay, be wholly precluded. It may be better to have counted visionary chickens, and not hatched them out, than never to have counted chickens at all. And perhaps it is what we may all have to come to, in time, however stoutly we have preferred the heard melody, while we could get it, to any unheard superior.

CHAPTER III

UP TO THE ALPS

—to reside
In thrilling region of thick-ribbed ice!
Measure for Measure, III. i.

I

The evil that wars do may live on long after the good has been duly interred at Versailles or some other seemly necropolis. Here, as I write, is another August slipping away to its close; morning and evening, sure as dayspring and Vesper, a boat train is steaming away out of Victoria station. "And I not there! And I not there!" as "Ionica" Cory sang of the fun that would still be going when he was dead. The gods or devils that rule over dollar and sterling and mark, as wanton boys over flies, killing one for their sport and preserving and fattening another, have once more settled our hash. Supreme as the roll of this planet, that stonily keeps down the rations of comfort for marmots and men, some remote Force to which we have not been wittingly rude has posted Cherubims to head us off from the Alps. It feels as if the earth had taken a heavy list to one side so as not to hold us up the right way to the sun.

This morning, if currencies had not gone to the dogs, partner and self might have been ringing the bell, so to speak, at the front door of heaven. The jocund dawn might have seen us leap from the train at Pontarlier, Vallorbes—the very names of the junctions are tuneful and fair; like Fontarabia, Vallombrosa, Bendemeer, they set horns blowing; they make roses swing in your mind. Our material part would be flinging itself in force on the buffet's thick-lipped white cups of hot coffee, our subtler essences would be drinking as deep of the outward-rippling folds of the forested Jura all round us, its pines kneaded up with the clouds; in the slow expulsive puffs of our engine, now shunting the Berne or Bale bit of the train away from the other bit, a new timbre would make itself heard, a kind of percipient sniff, a salute to the nimble high air. Lives there a man with nose so dead that, on one of those fine scenting mornings on which a holiday always begins, he could not smell the Alps from Mulhouse or Grenoble? The very engines of this world would shame him.

And then those lobbies and ante-rooms of the mansion of joy—the Swiss towns.

Ten years! And to my waking eye
Once more the roofs of Berne appear!

If only they did! Or those of Lucerne, or of Interlaken! Give us any the veriest seat of the "tourist industry"—whichever may be its Black Country's champion black diamond, its counterpart of our Widnes or Wigan. "Just let me get up again on to the earth," says a distinguished dead person in Homer; "better a sweated farm hand on a poky farm there than king of all the dead that ever died."

Faint and far the Jungfrau snows may be, as seen from the terrace at Berne; yet they are there; the beloved, if not in the room, is still in the house, a presence diffused and irradiant, animating the air of its chambers. But give us, if any choice between the dear seats of Philistine joy be permitted us, the Lake of Geneva. "Without my William," the enamoured maiden asks, in Scott's early poem, "what were heaven?" A gap even greater than Williamlessness—because it affects the happiness of a larger number of persons—is to be noted in many extant descriptions of Paradise. Nothing is said of a site for the Lake of Geneva. If this be no false alarm, many good Britons are in for a serious disappointment. On some the blow will have fallen already.

You may have seen the lake first on your way to Zermatt or Arolla or some other seat of the inner and major joys of the Alps. Perhaps you were apt at the time, in the pride of your youth, to speak a little cavalierly of Nyon and Vevey, Clarens and Montreux, with their Babylonish hotels, their pensionnaires and dress baskets, and cohorts of counts disguised as hall porters, and iron garden chairs beyond number, scrunching the dry greyish pebbles of terraces hot with massed magnolias and dahlias. Still, the train journey from Paris that day had been dusty and long: now, your first holiday dinner consumed, you possessed your soul in cool freshness and peace, smoking perhaps in the garden, lately laid waste, where Gibbon completed his stout attempt to put up something as durable as the opposite hills of Savoy. With a good show of stars overhead, and the glow-worms alight in the grass all around, and the lake, far below, all a-twinkle with lights fixed or shifting, it seemed pretty good to be there, even then. Or you had climbed hard for a month and came back, with all your exultant fitness astir in your muscles and mind, to eat your last Swiss meal at one of the balconied restaurants on the Grand Quai du Lac at Geneva, over the lapping water, before the train swallowed you up. Or you had half a day on your hands and passed it in cruising along the lake shore in one of the fat and inexpensive bourgeois steamers, dear to right-thinking men as the old Thames "peni-boat" was to the wise Vicomte de Florae, and contemplated in comfort the vestiges left by Ruskin, Voltaire and Rousseau. A goodly place, a goodly time.

II

Outer edges of old holidays, the marginal bits that you may have looked upon at the time as mere unavoidable selvage—these have a trick of waxing almost poignantly pleasant in recollection The true delight of travel, the one that is going to print itself unaccountably and indelibly on you, seems to prefer to come as a thief in the night, and not at the hours you specially fix for its entertainment. You make an appointment, as did Leslie Stephen, to meet it at sunset upon the top of Mont Blanc; or on the roof of Milan Cathedral at dawn; or you take a gondola far out on the lagoon at Venice, to look up and see sunrise strike the whole chain of the Alps; and, after all, the wayward spirit may only come at some moment and place that have seemed, till he does come, to have little distinction about them. Like other brands of happiness, this one can only be caught by hunting something else. Make for whatever thing seems to you best and this other will come by the way, if it chooses; the best-laid of holiday plans are rather like trees that you grow on the chance that a bird may sing, some day, on one of them.

This kind of indirect trapping of joy has always gone famously on by the Lake of Geneva. For one thing, the place is a portal; not, for the active traveller, a goal, but a means of entry to all the more strenuous and illustrious joys of the Alps and of Italy. Eagerness seldom does justice to portals at first. t is too keen to get through them. Only after some years of the sifting and reassessing that always go on n your memory does it come out that the gate may be almost the best part of some other things besides certain Cambridge colleges. And then it may be that, all unbeknownst, you are a better sheet of paper for printing visions upon, during your first and last hours of holiday. Mornings of coming home from school, mornings of starting on leave in the war, were times when the human spirit seemed to have feelers as long as an elephant's trunk, compared with their common nose-like extension.

And then, again, the Lake of Geneva is really, objectively, quite a delectable place, however much our haughty youthful hearts may have sneered at the tourist who never got any farther. Approached clemently and humanely, all the lacustrine devices of wooden piers in all sizes, ingenuous groves and grottos, bathing-sheds, frowning "castles," smiling cafes, all indescribably neat, have a winning, leisurely air; no flurried, hustling, competitive age betrays itself here; everything seems as if healthy and happy retired mariners, or the right sort of boys, must have made it and kept it going, for love.

Wherever you look, there is no break in this ingenuous trimness. Unlike the Alpine glaciers which Mark Twain reported to be so much more soiled by detritus in the Catholic cantons than in the Protestant ones, the Catholic southern shore has just the same expression of ardent dapperness as the Lutheran coast on the north.

III

Look upon Ouchy, "the port of Lausanne"; consider its pleasantness. The moment the traveller about to commit himself to the lake steamer at Ouchy alights from the little funicular train that has lowered him down the steep slope from Lausanne, and launches forth on the wide paved space that remains between him and the pier, he sees on his left a castellated pile. It looks, on the whole, as though it might have seen some forty summers, and imbibed two coats of paint in each preceding spring. In a certain measure it scowls, as a good castle should. And yet it almost audibly assures you that you must not take its scowl too seriously—you need not fear, for example, that it would disdain to receive you, *en pension*, towards the end of October, on terms unthinkable during the summer heats. This clement stronghold is the Hotel du Chateau; here slept, in the winter of 1922-23, the massed diplomacy of the Allies and of Turkey, then trying once more to adjust for a time the ever imperfect understanding between the Crescent and the Cross, or their several lay connections.

The Chateau, though still in the heyday of youth, and yet simulating the sterner graces of age, cannot fairly be called a whole and unqualified humbug. A bit of it is an authentic relic of the Middle Age. You can read it up in the venerable Dictionnaire Historique du Canton de Vaud. About the end of the twelfth century the bishop of the diocese seems to have piled up on the spot a kind of provincial Bastille. It was a wise pastor's precaution. He had some reason to fear that, if he lived too much in the open, the sheep of his flock might take to butting him, in requital for certain exactions, the perquisites of a shepherd. This safety appliance included a puissant donjon keep, a moat and an outer fortification garnished with towers. Safety first was the good prelate's care and, thus firmly entrenched, he and his successors collected harbour dues, fish and the like temporalities with unbroken success for over three centuries more. Then a stiff-necked laity grew weary of these tranquil fiscal relations. Concurring in a wide movement of the European mind, they cast their diocesan out of his citadel in 1536. Moutons enrages are proverbially dangerous.

Thenceforth the castle mouldered, serving divers base secular uses. Most of it fell to bits, but ancient prints of various dates show the donjon tower sticking up manfully among the ruins, right into the second half of the last century. Then at last it was restored, fearfully and wonderfully, to serve as a kind of patent of antiquity for the castellated hotel, which is built on the old castle's site. So there are quite enough blocks of twelfth-century stone in the building to give the susceptible tourist lawful vibrations of conscious contact with the Dark Ages—"those darling bygone times, Mr. Carker, with their delicious fortresses, and their dear old dungeons, and their delightful places of torture, and their romantic vengeances, and their picturesque assaults and sieges, and everything that makes life truly charming."

Wisdom was justified of her children. The Swiss are inspired hotel-keepers. Some centuries since, when a stranger strayed into one of their valleys, their simple forefathers would kill him and share out the little money he might have about him. Now they know better. They keep him alive and writing cheques. He has risen in economic value from the status of a hare or a wild pigeon to that of a milch cow—or, at the lowest, a good laying hen. And, to keep up his average yield, they diet not only body but soul; they melt heart-strings and purse-strings alike with cheap and cheery semi-gammon about Prisoners of Chillon, Tell's apple, the jousting of cows for the championship of the pasture, the prevalence of ghosts on the Matterhorn, and so on, till the lapse of coin from the wandering alien becomes almost spontaneous. The Swiss genius, at once intelligent, acquisitive and respectable, is fitly symbolised in an affair like the Chateau Hotel, where a little bit of the quite genuine thing is made to go an admirably long way in the stimulation of sentiment and custom. There, on the site where it took a mediaeval bishop—and he a baron besides—hundreds of armed men, a moat, and thousands of tons of masonry to collect a modest living from the neighbourhood, a competent hotel-keeper sits at ease to-day in an unfortified bureau. He is unpolluted with other blood than that of innumerable chickens and calves. And every summer liner from New York is almost an argosy of his own. It wafts him treasure unaccompanied by risk. It brings against his castle no beleaguerers but such as are mild and auriferous.

The Castle of Ouchy may well have become a somewhat cosmopolitan place while the recent peace-makers of Europe and Asia were earning their due beatitude in its beds and at its tables. It was not so in one old August of golden memory. Then it was wholly Columbian; at least the exceptions were insignificant. An Englishman or two strayed in at times to eat, sleep and take flight. And the waiters, perhaps, were the grave German diplomatists that they looked. And the physical air could, no doubt, be called Swiss. But in all the higher senses of the word the atmosphere was an import; the smoke-room an enclave of free American soil; the salle-a-manger richly endued, like an embassy, with the attribute of extra-territoriality; every saloon a detached snippet of some authentic Saratoga. Most of the English, ever enamoured of the carnal blessing of fresh air, affected the ampler garden and more windy bedrooms of the neighbouring Beaurivage. But still at each archaic casement of the Chateau a likely heroine for Henry James ate gums under the buff sunblind; the small American boy, of the kind that is raised as a guest in the hundred best hotels of two continents, ranged throughout the public rooms, reducing you to a gaping rustic with his devastatory knowledge of life; and the liberal parents of these notables gave bread to some of the last specimens observable in Europe of the old-time travelling courier.

IV

Let it not cast a chill on light-hearted youth if a passing mention be made of some few of the "historical and literary associations" to which the late Sir Frederick Treves, the arch-anti-appendicist of a generation ago, has done so much readable justice. From one extremity of the lake Calvin cast his reductive shadow over the naturally high spirits of Scotland. The little "New Town" at the other end must have entertained in its day some redoubtable custom, from Charlemagne downwards. About the middle of the northern shore Byron and Shelley put up at an inn which still wears the white lily of Baedeker's asterisk. At some other salubrious spot on the littoral Lenin remembered in exile some of the necessary parts of a practicable government, and forgot others. Among the delphiniums of Coppet the burning Mme. de Stael loved and sang, or at least got herself painted, by Vigee Le Brun, grasping a lyre amain with ostentatiously lyric intent. An inordinate number of dispossessed princes and kings, of pretenders unlikely to start, or sure, if they did, to start at long odds; of fallen statesmen, prima donnas retired, and runaway husbands and wives possessing some sort of distinction have cooled their heels and allowed their airy notions to mix beneficially with earth along the entire margin of the lake. An excellent place for the purpose, the whole of the foreground scenery being of the emollient or lenitive kind, as distinct from the inflammatory types—the Vesuvian or the notorious landscape of cypress and myrtle. But all this bookish part of my strain can be easily skipped by cheerful illiterates. "Jouk and let the jaw go by," as the Scots ballad says. Or all this associational side of the place may be kept pleasantly vague in the mind, as a sort of dim background not to be studied in too close detail, like the agreeably murmurous presence of numerous bees, no one of which you desire to handle more intimately. The Castle of Chillon can readily be avoided.

Turning over topographical prints and tasting the pangs of desire, one feels the old apprehension returning. "Heaven seems vara little improvement on Glesga," a good Glasgow man is said to have murmured, after death, to a friend who had predeceased him. "Man, this is no Heaven," the other replied. But what if the real abodes of the blest should admit of no looking south, as you swim in the warm shallows off Morges, to the Arctic snows basking in tropical haze on high shelves of the distant Mont Blanc? Not to walk again among the terraced vines of the Vaud, nor slide down the silent "string" railway between the rose gardens of Jordils; not to see any more the Chinese lanterns lightly swinging, each in its own surrounding bower of brightened green, among the acacia trees of Geneva quay gardens!—Vara little improvement on Glesga.

V

How long that beguiling lake can detain you, now as of old! But thought and desire run on to sunset tomorrow—the first bivouac at the edge of the snow, under the peak that my comrade and I had marked down as the next, just when the war came. For the five hottest afternoon hours we should have grunted and sweated up a vertical mile of turf and shale, boulder and snow, bent under our fardels of food and camp kit and fuel, maledictions no doubt on our lips and deep joy in our hearts. Now, our supper cooked and consumed, our tinware cleaned up and bestowed, our fire sunken into a quiet low glow, we should each be worming himself into his snug sleeping-bag, his boots deliciously off, his woollen helmet drawn over his head, neck and ears. There like the gods we should lie at our ease, with twilight Europe laid out below us. Up and up the snows of an opposite slope the edge of a field of rose-coloured light would swiftly withdraw. Five thousand feet under our perch a few bleared lights would begin to blink into sight, marking the highest habitations of man. Out of the darkling valley the sound of a big torrent down there would come up to us clearer and clearer as all the small day noises subsided; but round us the tiny head streams would be all falling silent, held up by the frost, infant Danubes or Rhines going quickly to sleep for the night under that muting touch. I think the night would be still, but very minute winds, clean and austere beyond words, would be leaping and pushing about here and there, making an infinitesimal whistling, and pressing the lightest finger-tips on the face. In the Great Bear, midway on his Autumn slant down to the North, the starry minutiae of head, foot and tail would be flashing with frosty sparkle.

Our bodies aglow with their husbanded warmth in the sacks, our faces glad of the cold like a skater's, these waking joys would pass into others. "He is not dead, but sleepeth"—can you quite truthfully say it of any one who sojourns by night in a kind of death-chamber or vault so curtained and stilled that its darkness is flat and toneless and all the right nightly procession of delicate sounds and skyey changes and modulations of light and of taste in the air comes to a dead stop as though the man were all but under an elm lid already? Sleep under the sky is seldom that utter withdrawal from life. Through some sort of film, some sort of feeler within you is still aware of the rhythmic murmur of existence; some unspecified part of your system keeps watch and reports to the rest that all's well; and yet you sleep all the more deeply, as infants will do when boughs wave overhead and the mail-cart is wheeled. Even if you should dream of the Devil and wake in a fright, you awake to things more fundamentally reassuring and guarding than that artificial black hush of indoors in which you strike matches and see the hands of your watch point to queer, half-credible places: Orion's sword is still hanging aright from his belt, as you and your million direct forefathers have known it; the moon has crossed, since you saw it, a normal, expressive stretch of the sky; all's right with the world.

Next morning the world would seem all frozen stiff in one piece, a single casting of iron—whenever a patch of ice in the nearest glacier, squeezed past endurance, made a desperate push to get on, the whole region would creak as if the great globe were breaking. And then, after that hard, that undeniably hard early meal—O, we give you scoffers the horrors of breakfast at that Arctic dawn—would come the active joys of the climb, the renewal of youth, the solution of care, the bath of sore souls, balm of hurt minds. Only one of the great writers seems to have known:

Carry your fever to the Alps, you of minds diseased; not to sit down in sight of them ruminating, for bodily ease and comfort will trick the soul and set you measuring our lean humanity against yonder sublime and infinite; but mount, rack the limbs, wrestle it out among the peaks; taste danger, sweat, earn rest; learn to discover ungrudgingly that haggard fatigue is the fair vision you have run to earth, and that rest is your uttermost reward. Would you know what it is to hope again, and have all your hopes at hand? Hang upon the crags at a gradient that makes your next step a debate between the thing you are and the thing you may become. There the merry little hopes grow for the climber like flowers and food, immediate, prompt to prove their uses, sufficient if just within the grasp, as mortal hopes should be. How the old lax life closes in about you there! You are the man of your faculties, nothing more. Why should a man pretend to be more? We ask it wonderingly when we are healthy. Poetic rhapsodists in the vales below may tell you of the joy and grandeur of the upper regions; they cannot pluck you the medical herb. He gets that for himself who wanders the marshy ledge at nightfal to behold the distant Sennhuttchen twinkle, who leaps the green-eyed crevasses, and in the solitude of an emerald alp stretches a salt hand to the mountain kine.

VI

Among mountains miracles happen with ease; the sun can stand still in the heavens and the dawn be undone and the sun that has set return to the sky. We went up through deepening twilight one midsummer evening to sleep at the hut beside the Orny Pass. Two hours' walk below the pass the sun said good-night. Far down behind us darkness filled the depths of the wooded Val Ferret. At nine o'clock we topped the Orny Pass to find time had turned back and the full pomp of sunset was burning russet and crimson before us, across the snowfield of Trient. I went the other way a few days after, leaving the hut on the pass at five in the morning. Up there the rocks and ice already glared in hot light; stones had begun to fall, for the lashings and bindings the frost had made fast for the night were being untied by the sun. As I glissaded down the glacier and the glen below it, the snow hardened under my feet, the sun passed out of sight, the village of Orsieres, below, was still involved in semi-night; I looked down upon un-vanished mist and obscurity and descended, as the hour advanced, into a pit of twilight that thickened and grew colder.

Why should such passages fill one's mind with so quick a rush of delight? Heaven knows. Perhaps they are Romance; it has been called the addition of strangeness to beauty. But why, indeed, should any of these sudden ravishments befall us, at the instance of things that we see? You know that swift, abrupt flood of enchantment:

Look! under that broad beech-tree I sat down, when I was last this way a-fishing. And the birds n the adjoining grove seemed to have a friendly contention with an echo, whose dead voice seemed to live in a hollow tree, near to the brow of that primrose hill. There I sat viewing the silver streams glide silently towards their centre, the tempestuous sea; yet sometimes opposed by rugged roots and pebble stones, which broke their waves, and turned them into foam. And sometimes I beguiled time by viewing the harmless lambs; some leaping securely in the cool shade, whilst others sported themselves in the cheerful sun—and saw others craving comfort from the swollen udders of their bleating dams. As I sat thus, these and other sights had so fully possest my soul with content, that I thought, as the poet has happily expressed it;

I was for that time lifted above earth,
And possest joys not promised in my birth.

Why, for the matter of that, should we fall in love, men with women and women with men, in whom most other people can see nothing to make any fuss about? Many, no doubt, will think what sorry gush these rhapsodies of the amateur mountaineer are; mere lover's rant. And yet every true lover has got hold of something of which he who has never had it can scarcely guess the worth. No lover has ever yet got it across the footlights to him who was never in love. To be rightly in love, to explore a new world, to discover Shakespeare—really discover him for yourself—to find yourself in the practice of an art, to achieve total absorption in some purpose not mean: these are the indefeasible good things of life; but also they are its in-communicables. To achieve any one of the list is to be shut up alone with a glorious secret you want to tell every one else. But all you can do is to wait and watch the divine spark falling on somebody, just here and there, by some sort of chance, far beyond your control, and not falling on others.

What could young Porphyro impel
To venture in the foeman's den?
What lore makes clear to us the spell
That sped the feet of Imogen?

Words fail you? So the mountaineer
Loves yon majestic dome of snow—
To him 'tis passionately dear,
As Juliet was to Romeo.

Who knows, fond questioner, how soon
On thee shall fall the sacred fire,
And thou on some great peak at noon,
Feeling, shalt need not to inquire.

That is to say, if those disordered exchanges should ever take a good turn. They say that the frequency of marriages has decreased tragically in England since Europe's business affairs fell into confusion. "Jack hath not Jill." So is it, too, with the snowy-robed Juliet of Mr. Yeld's excellent verse. One Romeo, to my knowledge, has not the fare to Verona.

CHAPTER IV

WHEN THE MAP IS IN TUNE

I am told there are people who do not care for maps, and I find it hard to believe.
R. L. STEVENSON.

I

It hurts to think of the pleasures that people turn away from their doors. There are some who have not even learnt to read maps. "Read" is the word mostly used, but "tune" would be better. For, till you know the trick, a fine map is about the nearest thing there is to a cunning instrument cased up, or, being open, put into his hands That knows no touch to tune the harmony.

Unless you are a mountaineer, an engineer, or a surveyor, the odds are that the great illumination will escape you, all your life; you may return to the grave without having ever known what it is like when the contour lines begin to sing together, like the Biblical stars.

Those contour lines are the crux. The beginner, the infant at this game, craves for a hill-coloured map, with its expressive coloured scale, from the lush green of alluvial meadows a few feet above the sea-level to sultry reddish-brown for Snowdon and the Cumbrian hills. Quite good things are they, too, in their way, as pretty nursery rhymes are good till you grow up enough to like Shelley. They give you fine vivid notions about the general modelling of a country. In fact we might want nothing more if the part of the earth's crust which stands up into the air were modelled like the part which lies under the sea. Of course the ocean floor is not flat. It has uplands and lowlands. But these rise and fall gently, in long sweeping slopes. Their low and softly undulating relief has been preserved in the sheltered peace of deep waters. That of lands exposed to the air has been everywhere lacerated and trenched, split up with wedges of ice, eroded by streams and battered and eaten by waves. So the irregularities of its surface have grown intricate and fantastic to a degree which cannot be fully expressed, on a map of practicable scale, by any system of colours that vary with heights.

Almost the same may be said of those masterpieces of the map-engraver's art, the best of our old hill-shaded Ordnance maps. In these you all but saw the actual slopes—at any rate the general slopes—of your hills and the tracts of high light along the ridges that they held up to the sun. Their summary of the make of a mountain mass, as a whole, is so vivid that to this day some of us prefer to walk the Derbyshire hills with no other map than this old thing of beauty, on which no railway is yet to be found threading Edale.

But no true epicure of the map will remain long content with these elementary pleasures. Soon he finds that both hill-tinted maps and hill-shaded maps have to stop where the real finesse of delineation begins. No tinted or shaded map of the English Lakes will tell you the true shape of Gillercombe or of Combe Ghyll, or distinguish the warty crown of Glaramara from Great Gable's regular dome. Only a few years ago our one-inch Ordnance map of Scawfell and its buttresses made the craggy north face of Great End look as if you could march a division of troops up or down it, big guns and all. There comes a time when the epicure craves for something at once more difficult and more richly stimulating and rewarding. He wants something on which to put forth his strength. And this he gets in any contour-lined map that is perfectly done. He gets it in some sheets, though not by any means all, of our one-inch Ordnance Survey. He gets it in a few special maps like the 1/50,000 Barbey map of the chain of Mont Blanc. Above all he gets it in every sheet of the glorious Siegfried map of Switzerland, the most wonderful representation ever given of mountainous land.

II

The maturing map-reader, planning his holidays in the hills, will now be able to know much more besides the height at which he would stand at any point on a fell path or on an open mountain side. The map will also tell him what he would see in every direction if he were there. The sensitively winding contour curves will show him from just what point on the Watendlath-Rosthwaite track the top of Great End will come into sight. They will show him whether, from Seatoller Fell, Helvellyn will be within view, or whether the intervening Armboth Fell is just high enough to blot the greater mountain out. A glance at the condensing or spreading lines should tell him which side of Scawfell is a crag to be climbed and which is a turf slope to be walked. Before he has ever tramped up Borrowdale or Greenup Ghyll he will know how much of the valley in front will be hidden by each jutting promontory of high ground on either side.

As in the reading of printed words or a musical score, precision and speed in the reading of maps can pretty rapidly be carried further and further. Soon the map is read, as it were, not word by word, but phrase by phrase; the meaning of whole passages of it leaps out; you see, with something like the summary grasp your eye would get of the actual scene, the long fa9ades of precipice and hanging glacier that there must be where the blue contour lines crowd up closely together right under a peak of twelve thousand feet, with a northern exposure, and also the vast, gently sloping expanses of snowfield below, where the lines flow out wider and wider apart, expressing broad shelves, and huge, shallow basins hoisted on upper floors of the mountain. A musician's mental ear, I suppose, can hear directly, when he reads a succession of notes on ruled paper, the rise and fall of an air, the jaunty lilt or triumphant rush or plaintive trail of its gait, its swelling loudness or shrunken whisper. So the reader of maps is freed, before long, from the need to go through a conscious act of interpretation when gazing at the mapped contours of a mountain that he has never seen. He no longer has to tell himself, as he cons the endless lines: "Where I see a succession of rising contour lines close together, and, just above them, a few lines further apart, and, above these, others close together again, it means that there is here a hollow in the mountain"; or "where the curvilinear contours change their course and all stab inwards pointedly towards the heart of the hill, roughly parallel to each other, make an acute angle, and then come out again to resume their old general direction, it means a deep, narrow glen or gully running up the hill-side." He has no more need to do that than you or I have to worry over the spelling and syntax of Keats in the "Ode to Autumn." The notation once learnt, the map conveys its own import with an immediateness and vivacity comparable with those of the score or the poem. Convexities and concavities of ground, the bluff, the defile, the long mounting bulge of a grassy ridge, the snuggling hollow within a mountain shaped like a horse-shoe—all come directly into your presence and offer you the spectacle of their high or low relief with a vivid sensuous sharpness.

III

Much enjoyment of these delights can generate in the mind a new power of topographic portraiture, a knack of forming circumstantially correct visions of large patches of the earth's surface. You learn, like a portrait-painter, to penetrate by the help of intuitive inference; you get at one thing through another. You see on a good map the course of the Mersey—short, traversing a plain for more than the latter half of its length; but also, in its head streams the Etherow and the Goyt, crossing rapid successions of contour lines in the Pennine moorlands of Longdendale and the Peak. You guess at once what the temper of such a river must be. For it is a very downcomer pipe, as a builder might say, in its upper course, to drain the steeper side of the much-drenched roof of the Pennine, from Buxton northward to somewhere near Oldham. Clearly a stream to be vexed with extravagant spates, swiftly rising and swiftly subsiding, before at last its pace wears itself out in the fat Cheshire flats, as the rushing and tearing Rhine of Bale slows down in level Holland. Then you examine the Mersey on your map, in the lowland reaches just after it works clear of the hills; and, with a happy inward crow of satisfaction you see, if your map is a thoroughly good one, how the stream is flanked throughout the many miles from Stockport to Sale with enormous flood banks raised to guard the riverain farms from just that termagant fury that you had looked out for.

Every educated person knows, in a sense, how the surface of England is modelled—how the formative ridge of the Pennine is dropped half-way down the country southwards like the firmer cartilage in the flesh of a widening nose; how the lateral bracket of the Lake hills is attached unsymmetrically to this central framework by the Shap bar, and so on. But few such persons conceive it with any imaginative energy or with the delight that such energy brings. The rest have the kind of knowledge that lies dead in the mind, as a classical education lies dead in the minds of most of those who have had it. It has to be raised from the dead by some evocatory miracle of appeal to the sensuous imagination—the kind of imagination that rejoices to take up and carry on the work of a bodily sense at a point where bodily sense can go no further. The work is carried on, at the best, with so much of the eager immediacy of actual sight, or hearing, and so little of the dusty cloudiness of common abstract thought, that on a peak of the Alps you may obtain a sensation almost indistinguishable from seeing with the bodily eye the whole structure of the Apennines, the Lombard plain and the silted Venetian lagoon, laid out under your eye. Or from a bulge of high ground in our Midlands, where the Nen, the Welland and the Bristol Avon rise almost together, you may suddenly feel that you see the whole complex of English rivers as sharply clear as you may see the rummaging roots of a bulb grown in a clear glass jar full of water.

These delights if you would have,
Come live with me and be my love.

Thus does the large-scale map woo the susceptible mind. Geography, in such a guise, is quite a different muse from the pedantic harridan who used to plague the spirit of youth with lists of chief towns, rivers and lakes, and statistics of leather, hardware and jute.

IV

Conscience murmurs here that I may be muddling in somebody's mind the distinction between pictures and maps. So be it clearly set down that painters and map-makers do not, or should not, attempt to give you the same thing as each other. Least of all will they do so when each is working his best.
It is true that the early eighteenth-century fathers of the British art of water-colour—as much the one and only wholly British art, by birth, as the good moorland grouse is the one and only wholly British bird—were topographic draughtsmen rather than artists. They worked for land-owners and rich antiquarians and other great folk who wanted no fanciful visions but "plain records of facts." They learnt their job, in the main, from certain artisans who for two centuries past had got work, off and on, at tinting maps and engravings "with gummed colours, but tempered very thinne and bodilesse," as one old writer says. The early eighteenth-century men made pencil drawings which certainly verged on sketch maps. These they ventured to tint very faintly, going at first but little beyond the sober palette of the makers of modern auctioneers' plans of estates up for sale. No doubt they went in godly fear of losing their situations if they should launch out in heavenly colours like the oil-painters.

Again, it is true that some of the old hill-shaded Ordnance maps, engraved as with genius, verge upon the sphere of influence of art, if they do not trespass upon it. Some of their representations of mountains are almost temperamental; they awe or exhilarate you with the sombre darkness of their mountain sides and the brilliant high lights of the summit ridges where you come into the sun; here, you feel, is a measure of success, which can hardly be unconscious, in rendering the mountain glory and mountain gloom.

And yet neither of these compromises between art and science achieves, or could achieve, final success. The art of the old timidly tinting topographers, men like Dayes, Hearne and Paul Sandby, is now seen to be of moment mainly as the childhood of something else, something that could not attain its own completeness until it came into the freedom with which Cox and Turner were one day to make it free. So, too, the old hill-shaded Ordnance maps can only strike us now as wonderful and beautiful attempts to do what is not possible. Maps are maps and pictures are pictures and never the twain shall meet; for the better a map is, and the better a picture, the more deeply do they differ in intention and in effect. A painter who is worth his salt will flatly refuse to give you just the precise physical facts of a landscape. It is not his business. His business is not to convey topographic information, but to express some emotion or other that he has felt in presence of that scene. Not fact, but his personal sense of fact; not the correct relative sizes of peaks that stand up round the head of a glacier, but some individual mood or quality of awe, perhaps, that possessed him and may perhaps have possessed nobody else that ever stood beneath that wall of wonder. To gain this end, he does, as a rule, bring into his picture something that may be made out to have some sort of likeness to what you or I might have seen from the point where he made his picture or sketch. In Turner's "Mer de Glace" you can undoubtedly discern a wild remote resemblance to certain physical features of the ice-fall leading up to the Col du Geant. At any rate, it is quite as like the Mer de Glace as it is like several other glaciers of the Alps. His St. Gotthard drawings, too, you might be rather more likely to identify with the St. Gotthard than with the St. Bernard or Simplon, if you know them all. But such resemblances are of little account. Turner clearly valued them little. He always threw them aside if they got in the way of his absorbing plan for expressing some grand excitement of his in terms which would win a way for it into the mind or heart of the right person looking at the picture. When one of his big emotions flooded him in presence of a black Alpine defile or a crumbling Border castle, the one thing for which he manifestly did not try was to make the public presently cry out, "How like it all is!" He treated crag and torrent, castle and forest and bridge, as so many freely transposable objects; he increased or diminished their comparative sizes as he thought fit; he moved them about and tried them in various relative positions, as poets shift their words about to make a line sound better; they and their sites and sizes, their make and texture, were no more to him than notes to be grouped at will into any chords that he might prefer for the working out of his tune.

So the most perfect of pictures may have no topographic value at all. As a guide to the traveller's feet it may delude and lead astray. Small blame to it. Guiding is not its business. So long as an artist is true to himself it matters little how false he may be to geography, geology or history. The Antony or the Macbeth of Shakespeare may well be completely unlike the original sinner bearing the name. Who cares? Perhaps both were dull men in the flesh; and, if so, what a mercy that Shakespeare has drawn them all wrong; their falsification was vastly worth while. If you know how to keep apart things that God has sundered, you do not go to Shakespeare or Turner for positive information about the lives or the measurements of the people and places that set their genius in action. You go to them for admittance into their personal confidence, not to find "the real Caesar" or get tips for worrying out walking routes in the Alps, but to be taken up for the moment into the state of wise and beautiful passion in which these rare creatures do their work.

Still, it is into another's passion that you are admitted by art. Not what you ever felt for yourself when gazing out from Richmond Hill, but what the spirit of Turner felt at the instance of that expanse of champaign and river; not your own inarticulate tumult of joy in presence of Tuscan vistas of cypress and poplar, but the serene, clear-running ecstasy of John Bellini before the same prospect, is what your mind apprehends and enjoys for some propitious instants. Quite distinct from that choice and fugitive experience is that which we commonplace people achieve for ourselves when confronted with nature herself. Each in his own poor way, we have to play Turner as well as we can, and make our delight or our awe articulate to ourselves in some selecting and composing reverie over such bits of the world as are ours to behold.

V

In nature a great landscape is nearly always rather bewildering. Even more than other contents of experience, it seems to bury us under the multitude of separate objects that it offers for our perception. Each detail that we see cries out to be separately observed. Their relations to one another, their several shares in the make-up of the scene as a whole, are more shy. They keep themselves to themselves. From any central peak in a great mountain range you see all round you a host of white points like the tops of trees in a thin forest when seen from the top of a tree specially tall. You may see nothing at all of that which makes the whole mountain range, unlike the more fortuitous aggregation of trees, a single organism or cunningly sustained arrangement, so that no drop of snow that falls on the tip of any peak will have trouble in travelling down an unbroken sequence of inclined planes, diversified with a few sheer drops, all the way to the sea. The scene, it may well be, looks grand, in a way, but capricious and baffling; its pell-mell profusion of grandeur may rouse in you little more than a kind of baulked willingness to admire, if you could but see it, the chain of dependence which runs throughout the whole physical world. There, when confusion threatens, the map comes in to your aid.

Its service, like that of a field-glass, is quite unemotional. Unlike all the arts, cartography leaves you to work up for yourself what emotion you may in the presence of Himalayas or Alps. It only offers to extend your power of perceiving what the physical elements of that scene are, how they are related to one another as causes or effects, and how their several functions take their places within the larger general function of a mountain-range as a moderator of rivers and a sculptor of lands. No first-rate map-maker attempts to "come the poet" over you. None tries to compound any atmosphere of august melancholy to fill his large-scale map of Venice, or of majesty and mystery for his sheets of the Central and East Pennine Alps. His line is "Feel anything that you like, or that you can. Your feelings are your affair, and mine are mine. I offer merely to enlarge your power of sight and of comprehension. I give you, not emotion, but a reinforcement of that basis of bodily sense and intellectual penetration on which some kind of emotion may or may not afterwards rest."

So to its other fascinations a great map like the Siegfried adds the fascination of a lofty reserve. It goes, to all appearance unmoved, into the most moving of places. The men who drew its higher glacier contours lived for weeks at a time in remote huts, or passed their nights in sleeping-sacks on rocks or the snow, under frosty stars. Thence they would go out to work when the pomp of dawn was beginning. The work was sometimes stopped by storms that made the steel of their axes spit fire and sing; all the claps of thunder and their echoes would become one continuous, undulant roar. They carried their loads of instruments and marking-stakes up and down hundreds of steps slowly cut in steep slopes of hard blue ice. Sometimes one of them slipped. After a tour of duty up in the snows, where your eyes come to feel as if their lids were cut off, the map-men would descend some evening to where greenness begins like a balm to hurt minds and the streams make happy little sounds among Alpenrosen. But not a trace of anything that they may have felt has passed into these austere records of theirs. There is one glory of the sun and another of the moon: it is great that what Byron saw of the Alps should have stirred him to break out in glorious rant about his own personal sensations among them; it is great, too, that a different breed of men should be content, by way of their work, to sink utterly everything that is personal to them in its doing, so that when the work is done and its reticent tale is at every one's service, no one asks

Who or what they have been
More than he asks what waves
In the moonlit solitudes mild
Of the midmost ocean have swelled,
Foamed for a moment, and gone.

Immense as our admiration must be for all who can talk to magnificent purpose about their own uncommon selves, one may admire, too, the magnificence of the unbroken silence of others. Thus utterly different from the artist, the map-maker fastens upon you in quite a different state of yourself. There is a time for yielding your mind to the passionate mood into which some great artist has passed at the instance of something that he sees: you melt with a luxurious self-surrender into the golden pensiveness of Vergil as he gazes at a river laving immemorial walls; or you sink back and bask, with a will, in the visionary lustre of Turner's "Dido Building Carthage" or the sad sunshine of Thackeray's Esmond. But there are times, too, when you will take your emotions at nobody's hand. You want now not to borrow but to make.

You are impelled to put forth directly upon what is around you whatever you have in yourself of the power of direct and independent feeling which everybody has in some degree, though it may only rise to momentous heights in a few people of genius. You wish to see, perhaps, the Alps or the English Lake hills through none of the beautiful kinds of stained glass that Byron and Ruskin, Turner and Wordsworth would interpose between your sight and these things "as they are," but through the glass, whatever its tint or its tintlessness may be, of your private temperament. And here the right map, explicit, exact and ungushing, seconds your effort.

"Things as they are"—the old phrase, no doubt is a trap. It implies some assumptions that seem to fade away into nonsense or nothing as soon as strict thought sets about its destructive work of analysis. Still, it may be used with due caution to signify those aspects of external things which fall under the jurisdiction of science rather than of art—all that can be measured, defined, referred to known causes and studied in its established effects. The phrase helps us to make clear to ourselves, so far as such clearness is not delusive, the distinction between our emotions and their objects, between our love and the beloved person, between fear and the enemy's attack or the storm's violence, between our own awe and the physical proportions of Westminster Abbey. Whatever philosophy may dissolve in the crucible minds of philosophers, we common people cling still to a working assumption that first there are things in existence outside our individual selves; that then we perceive them; and that, having perceived them, we then have, or may have, various feelings about them. The map is our friend at the second of these stages of approach to such emotion as we can muster.

It makes our perception go further, because it marshals into lucidity a mess of mixed, haphazard objects of perception. Into the inexpressive confusion which wide tracts of country present at first to the eye it brings an approach to simplicity and articulateness. It cannot be said that you are seeing as much from the summit of the Grand Combin, if you have no map, and can only see vague masses of black and white in the distance, as you see when you know that one high mass of white, about eighty miles off, is the Dauphine Meije, and that a low dark mass in the north is the Black Forest. Telescope, compass and map will all combine to extend your power of apprehending what you see. To love things you must know them, and these assistants will abridge for you the work of getting to know. By lightening that labour they leave your mind fresher and more full of spring, to put itself forth in the exercise of that curious mixed faculty which occupies a borderland between bodily sense and imagination, or between direct perception and creative thought. You may call it a trick of enhancing for the moment the subtlety and reach of a bodily sense. Or you may call it a knack of lending to imagined things an exceptional portion of the sharp and importunate reality of a piquant object of sense. It is that which brings all England into sight and stretches Europe itself out under your eyes like a map spread out on a floor.

CHAPTER V

ONE WAY TO GO ABOUT

He loved of life the myriad sides,

Pain, prayer and pleasure, act and sleep
As wallowing narwhals love the deep.

I

By the death of a friend a batch of old guide-books has come to be mine. He was much older than I, and the books were new in his youth; some of them even longer ago. There are early Murrays among them, visibly aimed at the young Briton of quality setting forth to make the grand tour; he needs hints about couriers and how to ride post across Spain and to get a little fox-hunting near Rome. Baedekers, too, of the time when Karl Baedeker, the founder of the dynasty, lived and liked plain food and a smoke, although he went from inn to inn like a king, investing the righteous with stars, and climbed the little Silberhorn, opposite Mürren, before any one else, as Baedeker's Switzerland bears filial witness to this day. The faded red Murrays re-plunge you deep in the long Victorian peace. They tell you how to go about to be invited to Court balls at courts which now "the lion and the lizard keep," or else the charwomen of some uneasily seated republic. One withered ancient speaks of the Papal States as of a kingdom of this world that can still ask for a passport and call people up to be taxed. At the top of each obsolete list of hotels, or not far away, you find a big Hotel de la Paix; wise husbandmen planted such fruit-trees during the sunny years when the long frost of the Napoleonic wars had broken up at last and the fertilising streams of pleasure travel were just beginning to run freely again.

It all sounds pretty old. Still, you feel the pride of up-to-dateness throbbing through the quaint print. In ancient photographs of mid-Victorian college groups you feel the same honest emotion charging with a melancholy charm the funny bowler hats of heroes now involved in endless night: some of them, no doubt, were gallants who then appeared to staid friends to be almost riding over the hounds in their absorbed pursuit of the latest mode. Murray, headlong fellow, rushes up with the news that M. Seiler, who keeps that excellent inn the Mont Rose at Zermatt, is putting up an hotel on the Riffel-Alp. Baedeker comes flying in to say that he has seen them making a cable tramway from Territet, on the Lake of Geneva, up into the wild hills of the hinterland, towards the Rochers de Naye. Breathlessly the great twin brethren keep abreast of hurrying Time, and of each other. Their older editions look stiff enough now, but what looks like an old codger now may well have been a regular Mercury once. The snows of yesteryear, quite the latest thing when they fell, might look deplorably demoded to-day if they had been, like stout octavo volumes, unable to melt.

Even the veriest youngsters of the company, striplings not published twenty years from to-day, contain pages that Time has clawed in his clutch, with results of some poignancy. The effect of war ruins, in general, upon a susceptible heart is notably heightened by this lacerating note on a Belgian tavern now lost to the world—"Good fish dinner on Friday." So that was one of the heaps of white rubble, that used to look, when you passed them by in the war, as though they had never been anything else—a place where the hearts of intelligent feeders, men of savoir manger, had beaten high with well-grounded hope during the earlier hours of countless Fridays.

Shakespeare was right: for pathos the detail is everything. "Indifferent and dear," wrote Murray, in his bluff Jehovian way, about another hotel that now has the nettles sprawling over its tumbled bones, a house on whose inconvenient garage and overcharging bureau you once felt a German bomb fall in the middle of dinner, like judgement striking down from a sky that had not previously looked angry. Does supreme justice, indeed, make use of these secular instruments? Were years and years of tepid soup, of unaired beds, and of unanswered bells holding, in some mystic sense, the joy-sticks of the venging Fokker on that April night? The wayward mind of man, ever seeking elsewhere a moral government of the universe in bulk, while he stoutly withholds this blessing from some of the little bits that he runs for himself, toys with that pleasant thought. Vain thought: naïf Old Testament thought, dispelled by the New. Had that other hotel-keeper peace—the just man that had the good fish every Friday?

II

Another little frailty of our nature comes out well in some of the old guide-books that sped our fathers to the Alps. This is the darling illusion about "desecration"—the feeling that every good place was just right as it was when we first consecrated it with our gaze, but that Goths, "trippers," "Cook's tourists," "Philistines," Vandals, etc., have been blasting it with their basilisk glances ever since, besides befouling it with their unsightly sleeping quarters and their graceless means of getting about. Do the angels collate this little trick of ours with our other little trick of crying "Lo!" here and "Lo!" there, when we see anything fine, and calling to every one else to look at it? If so, the angels' food for tears and laughter must be perceptibly improved. Here is Murray's Switzerland, eighteenth edition, crying out on the ugly hotel lately built on the Montanvert, near Chamonix. Murray's chaste taste mourns "the former modest inn," if not the still more ancient hut of turf and stones, where Saussure had slept under the lee of a boulder. But who were the real builders of that Montanvert hotel? Whymper, for one. His stone was well and truly laid the day he published that exciting narrative of the first climbing of the Aiguille Verte, across the way. Then Leslie Stephen, on the day when he made everybody want to see the sunset from Mont Blanc, or somewhere near. Then Tyndall, when he wrote his vivid, tingling stuff about his winter visit to the Montanvert itself, to measure the motion of the Mer de Glace. But always Murray, Murray, endless editions of him, all inciting to travel, and all the later editions telling people, and telling them well, how to go where Whymper, Stephen and Tyndall had gone. All these guilty creatures toiled to fill the Alps with crowds. You might think, as you go up by train to Zermatt, that the permanent way is composed of ballast and scree. Its surface certainly is. But this itself rests on a massive foundation of "Peaks, Passes and Glaciers," "The Playground of Europe," and "Scrambles amongst the Alps," and under all are several thick strata of successive issues of Murray's and of Baedeker's Switzerland.

Consider the case of the Col de Jaman, the grassiest cleft in the low mountain wall between the Bernese Oberland and the Lake of Geneva. Old travel diaries contain descriptions of the pass, the un-trodden turf aflame with yellow gentians, the tawny huts of a few cowherds cast away in wrinkles of the hills, the tinkling silence of pastures where mighty cows waded knee-deep in orchises and lilies through whole days of solitude, and then the sparkling surprise at the actual pass when the ground, all of a sudden, fell away from your feet to the blue glassy floor of the lake. That is the sort of thing, surely, to say nothing about, if you do not want Tom, Dick and Harry to come and deflower your Eden. But Byron happens to cross the pass. Straightway he blows the gaff. The view, the cows, the patriarchal pastorate, the Ranz des Vaches—he gives it all away. And then comes Murray and quotes from Byron in deep draughts. And then Matthew Arnold, to write a poem bewitching enough to send to the pass, and to Glion below it, any one not sent already by Byron and Murray. Last scene of all, that ends this comedy, Arnold comes back to the place some twenty years later, gives a start of dismay, and writes another poem:

Glion? Ah, twenty years, it cuts
All meaning from a name!
White houses prank where once were huts.
Glion, but not the same!

We should rather think not. But what had the man expected? That all his mellifluous verse, reinforced by the taut homespun prose of the Baedekers and Murrays, would not have brought one single whitewashed pension to the birth? There is a mountain railway to the Col de Jaman now; if pressed for time, you can see the cows from the train and buy the saffron gentians from little boys ranged in a row on the platform.

Still, we must not chide. We are all like Byron and Arnold, except in the detail of not having genius. "Each man kills the thing he loves," in this matter of undisturbed natural beauty. We find some picturesque nook-shotten Alpine hamlet, only to be reached by walking, or enduring the walk of a mule, for twenty miles; we write it up alluringly; we turn all the mountains round it into celebrated climbs; we annotate its inns and quote the prices of its homely merchandise; we inoculate England first and then Europe with the desire to see it. While doing this we may incidentally bid the baser sort of tourists avaunt. But that is only a form. That takes nothing away from the strength of the toxin that we inject. For nobody ever thinks himself a base tourist. Every one who reads us feels that he, too, is no clod, but one of the elect, pure in his tastes, made of air and fire, like the Dauphin's horse. So he goes forth to see. And then Babylonian hotels, jewellers' shops, light railways on the rack-and-pinion system must follow as the night the day. At last the great work is complete; a station of Cyclopean build is flouting the sky upon the Gorner Grat; specimens of all the richer nations of the earth, with their long dress-baskets, are being hauled up steep shoots by wire ropes to the eyries for which we have taught them to long. But do we sing "Nunc dimittis," or say "Behold, it is all very good"? Not we. We cry out that the Philistines are upon us and we must go somewhere else. Like the novelists' heroines, we have a charming inconsequence.

III

Is it, then, that the Arnolds and Byrons seriously ought to keep their discoveries dark? And a Wordsworth say nothing about Helvellyn or Rydal? And Turner not paint the Rhone Valley brimming with cloud, nor express the awesome ticklishness of the old ledge track across the St. Gotthard. Murray and Baedeker too—should they disdain to assist in bringing the vulgar in to trample the lawns of Paradise? No; reason rejects the idea; it is fantastic. A place, like a person, must take the chances of life as they come. If it is great it must face the normal troubles of greatness.

Almost any sequestered and yet accessible place which eloquent people trumpet into celebrity has to go through a sort of lifetime, complete with its successive ages: first an infancy, or something a little colder perhaps—a misty dawn with the grey beading of dew still cool on the un-rubbed bloom of fruit in a walled garden out of the way; then a long passing away, by degrees, from that auroral and inviolate reserve into successive stages of tarnish and heat—boyhood and hobbledehoyhood, followed, perhaps, by a golden or gilt prime of worldwide fame and roaring business, and then by Heaven knows what, for we don't? What will become of Zermatt when there are lifts up all the peaks and buffets at their tops? People may come to have had enough of it then. Later on, they may go to the place, yet again, as we go to Pompeii, just to see the queer things that we did in the places we went to for fun. Who knows? Mr. Hardy's prediction, by then, may be coming out true, and people be finding wide wastes of wet sand more grateful to their sobered minds than the evening roses that creep up the snows of the Valais and crown the cup of our own headier rapture. An August tour up the Rhine, among castles and vines, seems to have been, to our guileless grandsires in their youth, the last word in romantic felicity. Us too it may move, but mainly because of its documentary quaintness; it ranks with the baby rattles of kings who grew up to lose kingdoms, or sticks of the rockets that used to go up of a night at some vanished Vauxhall.

Well, nothing can live for ever. We must be satisfied. The loveliest place, like the loveliest face, has to age, and Matterhorns are ripening towards decay as surely as apples and oaks. The Alps are all falling to ruin, the Sistine Madonna is fading, Leonardo's "Last Supper" is gone, the glass of York Minster is rotting away. But, in a world that spins always more slowly round a sun that is losing its heat, we may well acquiesce in these minor examples of the ubiquity of impermanence and even in the irony that makes us so eager to hurry our freshest delights on into the dust to which they are in any case consigned.

Besides, there are great consolations. A strong illusion protects us from panic, at least for part of our time. If one could really understand in youth the quiet ticking of one's watch, and know it to be, in sober truth, the perpetual dripping of irreplaceable waters of life, most of them poured out to waste upon sand, one might go mad or run wildly this way and that, crying "What shall I do? What shall I do?" But nature has excellent plans of her own to work out, and capital blinkers to put on the eyes of such creatures as seem to work better blind. And so things appear, to our sense, to stand still for a while, as if at a glorious climax; no garden that we knew as children could be thought of, then, as either older or younger than it was; and now Mont Blanc is, to us, no mere middle term in a series of blastings and levellings—just as it stands it is for our eyes a masterpiece finished, carved to the last touch, and eternal; for this the world has lived; and any earlier states of the earth were only steps leading up to the present divine consummation; any later states that may come can only be fallings away, gaps like the ones made by the failing of teeth or the deaths of old friends; the fall of the beech from which your swing hung when you were a child can never look like part of a growth or progress. For most of us, in our inmost thoughts, do not seem to stand midway up a long slope of time, but right at the top, as if on a hill, with the past and the future both falling away from our feet, and both declining in interest as they go.

See a great fire, how the flames pass from shape into shape, lambent and aspirant plumes, poised or waving, some open like fully-blown tulips and some pursed to a point like shut daisies, but all vanishing as soon as formed and none recurring just as it was. All experience burns away like that. To be able, or seem to be able, to fix the forms of a few of its momentary flames, to fall in love with them and hug our own vision of their beauty and give that image a place in the abiding dream about ourselves, the gallant, swaggering or maudlin dream about ourselves, which each of us keeps going in some secret place in his mind—this faculty is both our help and our disablement. One of nature's purposeful lies, it pro-vides the calm that we need, as well as courage and pride, in order to work while yet it is light. And yet it may lull too completely our sense of the coming-on of an extinctive evening, so that all that many of us do with our single chance, our one day, is to get a sense of some few glamorous and enchanting things that seem as if they might last, and then to be overtaken by twilight, with nothing done. But even to get that impression, in all its sparkle and lustre, is something. In quite a few years we may seem to have counted for nothing more than the then invisible cause of a place polished smooth on the back of a chair. And yet the stores of the race may have been minutely enriched if we have not returned, as Grumio says, un-experienced to our graves.

IV

Can there ever have been such a time as the generation before the war, for sunning yourself in the warmth of that kind illusion? Europe lay open to roaming feet as it had never done before and never has done since. You did not even need to have much money; money went twice as far as to-day; it went as only shells go now. All frontiers were unlocked. You wandered freely about the Continent as if it were your own country. Plenty of us had pervaded at any rate France, Italy, Switzerland and the Low Countries for twenty or thirty years without knowing what a passport looked like. The thing had first become an obsolete nuisance, like the appendix or some other bodily gland that has outlived its function—a thing to cut out. Then it had passed into a joke; quaint people in spy melodramas at second-rate theatres seemed to have passports, but nobody else. Baedeker, certainly, said that a passport, presented in a Swiss post office, might help you to get your registered letters. But Murray considered it better, in case of doubt or dispute, to present a cigar.

Europe had come to feel that fussing with broken bottles on walls belonged to a period before sanitation was born. A mediaeval immigrant might, for all that you knew, be sickening with the Black Death, or else with some moral ailment equally fatal. The only prophylactic of which mediaeval Europe could think, besides praying and promising to build a church, was to make it a tough job for the man to get in at the door. An early quarantine instinct persuaded the good people of Tudor Dover to chivvy the disembarking alien to his hotel with hoots and menacing cries of "French dog!" A mangy dog, perhaps. Failing carbolic acid, ovations like this were a means to limit one's perils.

England, ever in the van of the plumber's trade, worked off pretty soon her faith in these rude precautions. She grew to make a regular hobby of letting any one in who knocked at the gate, and no questions asked. She never bothered Victor Hugo for his papers; Louis Philippe and Louis Napoleon, Mazzini and Panizzi, Kosciuszko and Kossuth and Marx and Kropotkin, Dom Manuel and Louis Blanc and Tchaikowsky, all folded their wings on our shores at the end of their various tempestuous flights, without any sort of ado. "All foreigners and beggars come from God," says somebody in Homer. England took a modest pride in acting as if she had read this and thought it was true.

The rest of Europe noticed, with some surprise, that England did not perish in her folly. Indeed, we were less stabbed and bombed than Continental Europe herself by activist political thinkers; our sovereigns continued to observe their modern habit of dying in bed; Britannia did not even have to keep on her person such chartered lice as secret police. And so at last old habit loosened its hold upon the European mind. Switzerland saw that a land of large, attractive hotels is the better for not having any barbed-wire entanglement round it. The Germans and French, with their fine business instinct, perceived that the energies of commercial travellers can be more gainfully used in soliciting custom than even in interviewing consuls, construing rules and by-laws, or expiating their infringement. At last the millennium was well under way. At any rate it had not been called back, as yet, from a false start that warmed the heart while it lasted. By 1890 a man, or even a woman, whose luggage would go in the rack, could traverse West and Central Europe almost as freely as a vagrant wind.

That was the time to be young. And many men young at the time had the wit to know it; the luck, too, to be able to act on that knowledge. Where mis-education had not killed out some natural liveliness of brain there often grew up a habit of travelling Europe with all one's youthful perceptions eagerly at work. It seemed spiritless not to have seen, if you could, what was left of all that Florence and Aix-la-Chapelle had meant for the world; why not see for yourself the death-bed of Athens in Syracuse Bay, and track the feet of Hannibal and of Charlemagne over the Alps? Men put their curiosity to school in the galleries and the churches of Holland and Rome, and sometimes of Petrograd and Madrid. Some were not even ashamed to have teachers; they looked at the "Gioconda" in the Louvre by the soft light of the lamp that Pater had lately hung over it, or they lay supine on the floor of the Sistine Chapel and willingly searched for such things as Ruskin seemed to have seen in the frescoes above; they trained themselves with a will to draw from the echoing stillness filling the choir of Beauvais and the nave of Amiens, from the lustrous repose of the guildhalls of Brussels and Bruges and the poignancy of the derelict arches that cross the soundless Campagna, whatever of exaltation, geniality or awe the sight of these marvels can still stir in the mind and heart.

Of course they were not pundits: no mortal embrace can take in, with circumstantial fullness of comprehension, so many vast things. Of course, too, there were pilgrims that failed by the way, and turned into pedants, superior persons and prigs of all the known tribes. Every industry has its by-products, and some of them rubbishy. Still the staple results were such people as make a country first-rate and keep the precarious channel open along which there trickles from century to century the thin, impeded stream of fineness in all the arts. The best of them tried, humbly and hard, to live among big things and not be dolts, to de-provincialise their minds and to stand at the centre and get at the standards by which a Giotto, a Bach or a Shakespeare would judge the next thing he saw. And the quest of this grail, like other hard exercise, helped to keep the soul fit. A man or woman taken with the glimmer of glories like these, on ahead, is immune, as a rule, from many ignoble maladies. Squalid fears and desires, timid gregarious instincts, the empty person's importunate craving to "have a good time" in some poor slavish sense of the words—these are likely to shrivel away in the heat of the more generous passion.

V

My friend had been of that lusty breed. Abrupt, zestful notes in the margins of these his old guide-books express him. They bring him back in his great mental, and bodily strength, a man of sudden roars of laughter, big gestures and bursts of high gusto, full of sense and boisterous humour, scholarship and un-bookishness. I figure him early in the 'nineties, counting up his cash about Midsummer Day, in shabby lodgings at Oxford. He settles it; yes, it will just run to four weeks abroad, in the deeps of heaven, his feet on Umbrian or Tuscan ground and his head among the stars. Or he comes into sight on the Riva, in Venice, going to glory in Carpaccio paintings all the hot morning under the Schiavoni church's low brows, and then off in the afternoon, like a schoolboy released, for a great swim at the Lido. Or else at Ravenna, legging it out along the tropical road through the malarious marsh to the pinewood beloved of Boccaccio and Dante. Or fallen in love at Milan with the grave, gentle mind of Lorenzo Lotto and rushing south, past Rimini, to woo it in the churches of bleak Ancona—and there to see by chance some dirty and lovable collier from Durham unloading under Trajan's white arch and hard by the columns that Juvenal saw in the temple of Venus perched on the cape; and thence making westward by road, for cheapness, irresistibly beckoned across the rain-soaked Apennines to walk himself footsore, in trances of gleeful absorption, among the jumbled wonders and bewilderment of primitive, Imperial and Renaissance Rome; or to sit in late evening sunlight alone in the ancient open-air theatre dug out on the hill above Fiesole, the finches hopping from bench to bench round him, the wooded heights mantling greenly above, and the Arno valley, a vessel now filling with depth below depth of rose-purple, darkling below—all the visible world as fair as the descant written in its honour in the book that lies open on his knees:

Every moment some form grows perfect in hand or face; some tone on the hills or the sea is choicer than the rest; some mood of passion or insight or intellectual excitement is irresistibly real and attractive to us—for that moment only. Not the fruit of experience, but experience itself, is the end. A counted number of pulses only is given to us of a variegated, dramatic life. How may we see in them all that is to be seen in them by the finest senses? How shall we pass most swiftly from point to point, and be present always at the focus where the greatest number of vital forces unite in their purest energy?

VI

But perhaps this hungry traveller was most wholly himself in some dominant parts of the Alps. Where his old "Murray" approaches one of these cardinal points, the notes in the margin thicken; they point in one direction; they close in. You see the man's inclinations feeling their way towards something that draws and excites them, but has to be found. And then you see he is there.

The place he has reached is, as nearly as may be, the vital centre of Europe. Here is the physical heart, the power-house, the cistern and the head scavenger of at least the western half of that large region. From one small patch of high rock and snow, taking up a few square miles, are sent down all the great rivers that during historical times have run like main arteries through the body of Europe, governing the distribution of peoples, directing the routes of their commerce, financing civilisations, enabling cities to be founded, and deciding wars. From a point not far from the St. Gotthard Pass the head waters of the Rhine, the Rhone, the Po and the Danube are all within the landscape that you see. Here you are placed at a seat of command whence there radiate the wires that give order and animation to armies too great and too widely deployed to be seen with the bodily eye at one time. From here there go about their multifarious business the threads of governing force that are not to rest from their august patrol of Europe till they obtain their discharge into seas whose other sides are America, Africa and Asia.

To see Nature holding so many reins in one hand gives a wonderful lift to your mind. All going well, it is lifted into that rare and happy state in which the senses seem to borrow for the moment the longer range of imagination, or else imagination borrows the vivid urgency of bodily sense. As you muse on each stream and its course, the touch of your mind, like the touch of the spider in Pope, "feels at the thread and lives along the line" till things far out of sight come excitingly near to its physical borders. Nature herself may awake into an all but visible person, sitting apart in these austere headquarters where no stir is felt but that of a few of the biggest forces that she employs in her administration of the earth—gravitation and frost and the sun, the falling and melting of snow. Artificer and ruler, you almost feel her to be seeing from here, as with the eyes of our body, all that she governs and everything that she makes. You yourself, as if admitted into some creative ecstasy of vision, begin to see it too. Like a Blake discovering the world implicit in a grain of sand, you seem, at least for a few divine moments, to see out to the end, with the exciting sharpness of sense, the declivities beginning at your feet; and with them all the voluminous sweep of the Danube and Rhine past Cologne and Belgrade, and the fan-shaped cloud of dull grey projected out over the blue Adriatic below, where the Po is still laying down in the sea the same glacier-ground silt that shallowed out the Venetian lagoon.

Once lifted into that transport of exhilarated sense or of imaginative thrill, you can, for the moment, understand anything. You see with ease the causes and the working of many intricate things. The doings of nature fall, of themselves, into luminous order; you view them in all their inevitable and bewitching coherence; facts that had been, for you, no better than disparate data of separate arts and sciences— points of history, myth, geology, botany—suddenly become members one of another; they give each other their rights of completeness and causation; the early autumn glow of mulberry and walnut woods below you to the south declares the makings of Titian and of Tintoret; the grey chill sinking down already on the darkling pines of Northern Europe, when you turn to look where the Black Forest lies, makes you one, the next moment, with overcast souls that carved themselves congenial refuges among the warm, ruminative glooms of dim Gothic cathedrals, and worked out grim "Dances of Death" by way of a stoical humour to keep up their spirits through the long winter darkness of mediaeval Nuremberg or Lucerne. Why Holland is flat and Italy poor; why Luther prevailed where he did; why Germans and French are never at peace, and Belgium always a cockpit; how throughout all the racket or rhythm of Christendom's career the quiet brown bear has been drawing slowly back across Europe along the strip of failing cover that once was a broad band of forest and mountain running through Pyrenees, Alps and Carpathians, from the Atlantic all the way to the Caucasus; how the vine traces a line of its own across the frontiers of States and tints a map of Europe for itself, tinging the lives and songs of peoples with its dyes—these and a hundred facts bigger than these you no longer merely remember, but see: they take life; they are made flesh, like the Word; they shine out in endless new connections, near and far; they rush triumphantly to help each other into radiant clearness in your sight till you feel as the man may have done who said that once the stars sang together and all the sons of God shouted for joy.

Some of the old writers write about Knowledge with passion, as lovers speak of a mistress. She is "divine"; to "woo" her is rapture; to win her is joy past words. That is the tone, and to the common run of our middle-class young to-day it must seem to be mere tall talking or gush. For they are out of it all; it belongs to a lost world which they are not even able to miss, they are so far from having ever entered it. Checked in their mental growth by dead mechanical teaching, bound over for life to remain overgrown dunces, tied down to second-rateness by many impressionable years of intimacy with mean valuations, what are the poor things to do? Some of them are brought, perhaps, by the more virile kinds of sport as near as they are likely ever to come to the thrill of the high adventures of the human spirit. Some others put up with such simulacra as dissipation affords of the most puissant emotions attainable by men. Some just eddy about in the eddying dust all their days, blown round and round by adventitious gusts of sentimentalism or of fashion.

But some do escape. Hardy souls, they face with a will the risk of taking a way of their own; they make a break for the freedom that comes to the bold wooer of knowledge as well as to the true lover in Lovelace's poem; they go blithely on with the task that was set them long before they were born—to re-live for themselves the whole life of man, re-explore his world and re-discover his arts. Happy those of them who had their youth—as many had who were not to have much more—in those unhampered years before the war came to chill and constrict what it did not destroy. The covers of their Murrays and their Baedekers have faded, rather like Ophelia's violets that withered all when her father died. But the redolence stays. It is that of a time when a view of the whole of the larger life of our race, the life in which the greatest things are felt or found or made, had come to be almost any one's for the asking. For the moment the key of the garden hung by the gate: you had only to reach for it.

CHAPTER VI

ANOTHER WAY

If all the year were playing holidays,
To sport would be as tedious as to work.
Henry IV. Part I. I. ii.

I

If you take a dog out for a walk you will see him hastening from one selected point to another with an air of "extreme eagerness. To each he addresses his nostrils seriously. Then he speeds on to the next as if every moment were his last—before life fails he must put forth the strength and the refinement of his nose upon the enthralling fragrance of all the choicer ingredients of life.

Whole campaigns of seemingly impassioned sniffing are thus prosecuted. For, surely, the business must, like a campaign, have some sort of cohesion; a dog of parts cannot be always accumulating mere odoriferous data, mere isolated and disparate facts; some elements of a philosophy must emerge; some rude culture, some infant critical system.

In such a dog the memory must presently resemble a room hung, in some order or other, with etchings of persons, places and leading events—every print a smell, every line a contributive whiff. Novels say that a drowning man, at the moment of his departure, lives through all his past days again. If so, what chords, fugues and canons of perfume may have thronged for one supreme instant the gifted nostrils of the unfortunates sometimes observable in our canals and ponds. Think, too, of what may pass when two aged dogs, aromatists of the old school, meet and communicate. "Vieille hole, bonne hole, begad!"—of course they share that tender sentiment with Major Pendennis and all God's other veteran creatures; Caesar must signify somehow to Luath that Ponto's extinction last week has severed one of the few links that remained with the dear dead days when a smell was a smell; and Luath no doubt would call up, with some reminiscent flick of the muzzle, the fine collectorship of the dead, the fund of choice aromas hoarded in his memory, and his exquisite sense of relative values in various scents. "He was a dog, take him for all in all, we shall not ever smell his like again."

II

This pitch of assiduity in the employment of any one sense is not easily attained by man. Still, an approach has been made by some American and English persons of an advanced culture. Released from the cares of this world they have given themselves, as whole-time devotees, to the snuffing up of the immemorial odours of charmful places, their distinctive essence and characteristic appeal. The war may have thinned them out. No doubt it somewhat changed the personnel of the corps; for it redistributed wealth, and aromatists have to be more or less wealthy. It must at any rate have discommoded them. The fifty years before it were their great time for maturing, that being Europe's season of greatest wealth and easiest transport and least discourtesy all round. France, from Paris southwards, knew the breed; specimens were to be seen in the older German and Austrian towns; the Prado drew some to Madrid; the Hermitage took others to St. Petersburg. But Italy was the place; to various degrees of density the whole peninsula was speckled with highly civilised aliens who had contrived to convert our intractable life into one elegant and exquisite holiday. We others, plain working-folk taking a month's rest from our labours, would find them in permanent occupation of Florence, Bologna, Perugia, Assisi, a little faint at times with sheer excess of masterpieces, but still pursuing. Or in the Alps we would meet them in summer, when they had fallen away for the moment, fully charged and slightly lethargic, like the mosquito after his meals, from the year-long fruition of beauty and ancientry; there they would give their o'er-laboured noses a total rest, amidst the salubrious vacuity and nullity—for all the higher purposes—of peak and glacier, before these delicate corporal agents were bent up once more to the strenuous enjoyment of the perfumed past.

Do not confuse these devotees with people who go to live on the Lung Arno or over the Grand Canal in order to write learned or sensitive books, or to bottle atmosphere for a novel, or else to screw themselves up to the needful point for emitting authentic poetry. A Browning may live in a large Renaissance palace at Venice by way of his trade; he sucks up local colour industrially, much as a hound inhales the scent of a fox, or a specialist pig absorbs the faint, fine odour of truffles. To each the congenial redolence is so much raw material for his professional toils. Doubtless all the three animals like it. But that only shows that each has found his vocation and not that they are mere animals of pleasure. The whole-hog aromatist is. From him nothing of household use, such as a poem, the brush of a fox, or a good truffle, proceeds. He just, in the highest and purest and most intelligent sense, but still quite unproductively, sniffs and sniffs and sniffs again, like our friends Beppo and Rover on their walks. Rich enough not to bother, cultivated up to the nines, undistracted by family duties, or abdicating them freely, good aromatists turn from the relatively infragrant lands of their birth to live in the pink jails that pass for villas in Piedmont or in mouldering masterpieces of Lombard Gothic. They cast from them, for ever, even those lighter pursuits of the chase or the board-room which almost convince the British squire or guinea-pig that he does some sort of work in return for his rather expensive keep. They leave all, just to exist intensely as so many perfected systems of perceptions, persistently stringing like beads their countless smooth round days of receptivity in galleries, churches and squares, in Boboli and Pincian Gardens and along the Appian Way, always quickening and re-quickening their discriminant sense of some distinctive quality in this or in that—in the bespangled and twinkling Ravenna mosaics, in Botticelli's piquant betrayals of sceptical lassitude or in the startling wild grace of Donatello, in John Bellini's great love or Luini's capital sugar. There they are, a standing public for the quattrocento, a "gate" for the Renaissance; while they subsist, the last enchantments of the Middle Age, whispering from Giotto's tower and Brunelleschi's dome, are sure of an audience that has its receivers properly tuned.

III

Some of them were baffling company for us plain souls. They would practise astute refinements of pleasure that we had not thought of. Only in certain moods of one's own, they would say, should certain places be seen. It was mere bungling and waste to address oneself to the whispering Umbrian peace of Perugia in the key of urbane animation congenial to Florence—poor old Florence, now so overrun. Only a clown would bring to Sorrento the trailing mood of melancholy that gave Venice—the Venice of twenty years since—its fullest value for sensitive souls, or accost the lingering sunshine and the crumbling walls of that lost Venice in the spirit of delicate epicurean positivism propitious to a proper absorption of the essential Neapolitan savours.

These leaders of the march of taste seemed always to have just discovered some quintessential new essence of charm, some real right thing which we ought to have heard of already, but hadn't. They used to leave us standing, just when we thought that we had all but caught up. Venice, it seemed, was all very well, but did we not know that the last distillation of the basic spirit of her early life was to be caught at—O no; not at Torcello; poor old Ruskin might have fancied that—but in some squat rural slum on the mainland; or else among those drear, bald quays of northern Venice where nothing is fair to outward view and where starved fish-mongers rend your heart by opening shop for the day with a stock of two flounders and an infant eel? Or we might hear that Giorgione—Giorgione for love of whom we had just walked on pilgrimage through dust and flaming sun to Castelfranco—had talent no doubt, but, after all, what was he besides this new pupil of Titian's "that everybody is talking about"—you know that august invisible "everybody" who is quoted by the elect—a veiled prophet, a voice from a curtained shrine? Far ahead we seemed to discern these tall captains bearing into strange new fields of conquest the banner of critical assurance, while we enjoyed ourselves ignobly among the spoils of its older campaigns, lying upon our Philistine backs on the floor of the Sistine Chapel to adore Michelangelo's frescoes, or gaping in rustic delight at the Giottos at Padua, or ravished with mellow-seeming but doubtless naif reflections about mortality in the quiet Campo Santo at Pisa, in spite of the stars with which Baedeker had made vieux jeu of these stock sources of agreeable emotion.

Others, more merciful to men of mould, could belong to the higher race and yet cast no basilisk eye on the ingenuous joys of relatively untutored travellers. Their more catholic minds disdained no savour, so long, perhaps, as its date was before 1600. However strongly guidebooks might praise it, however densely tourists might throng round to inhale it, they would not deny nor forsake it. No ingredient that had entered into the immense pot-pourri of mediaeval Italy was mean in their nostrils. These, in truth, were most like the arch-aromatists whom I first spoke of. For your perambulant dog, however enamoured of some impossible perfection that always illudes him from just round the next corner, is still catholic. When did any dog turn up his nose at a smell—unless, of course, the smell itself was rising richly from the ground into the air. Tout comprendre est tout pardonner; he investigates all and he calls none unclean or common, not even the ancient and fish-like, as it may seem to the jaundiced sense of those of us that have not love. Times are, indeed, when smelliness pure and simple, quantity rather than quality, just the ineffable affluence of Nature's bounty to the nose, seems to ravish one of these great lovers almost clean off the earth. See him espy a flattish piece of carrion decomposing in a field. He rolls himself over and over upon it in ecstasy—doubly intense if a recent bath and the impoverishing action of soap have left the scent of his own personality noticeably jejune. At intervals he will arise and twirl round and round on his quadrupedal base, as they say that the dervishes do when they too are powerfully inspired, his whirling nose still pursuing and reviewing the fund of perfume already adhering to his whirling haunches. Then to it again, rolling on back and sides, to secure, in this fugitive season of plenty, an adequate store of portable material for the future exercise of the divine faculty. With some such ecstasy, some simulacrum at least of such ecstasy, would the more robust and more humane of our aromatists roll themselves in the Renaissance at large or plunge their noses deep in the full rosebowl of the quattrocento.

IV

I had a friend of this kidney whom fate, in its cruelty, forced to return for some months to England, his poor country. Some aromatic place to live in had to be found at short notice. Stratford-on-Avon occurred to his mind. But only as a passing thought; Stratford was vulgarised now; Shakespearean fragrance was too unmistakably merchandise there; it was like the "priest's hole" that the auctioneers vaunt when trying to sell a country house, or one of the numerous trees scaled by Charles the Second after the battle of Worcester, or of the many endlessly advertised bedrooms slept in by Queen Anne, or the public-houses at which a king has drawn rein. His chaste choice fell at last upon Richmond, in Surrey. It drew him the more because the loud impertinence of fashion no longer pestered the place; the Victorian custom of driving down from town to dine on summer evenings at the Star and Garter was over; no worldly Pendennises came out now to dine on the hill,

Not wholly in the busy world, nor quite
Without it.

Richmond had seen its own vogue come in and go out, and now it had turned to rest again and inhale its own respectable Araby of historic perfumes.

In a proper spirit of reverence for the past my friend took furnished—with seemly furniture of its proper period—one of the four small but beautiful houses which George the First built to lodge the maids-of-honour of his heir-apparent's wife. His back windows gave upon a surviving piece of the palace where Katharine of Arragon received the first news of Flodden. Early on midsummer mornings a small portion of shadow was cast upon his front garden by the cedars surrounding the house in which, it is rumoured, Queen Elizabeth died. Outside his front gate, an exemplary piece of Georgian iron, there lay Richmond Green, whereon it is held that Alice Perrers figured at a tournament, temp. Edward III., as Lady of the Sun. Two hundred yards to the south of his back garden wall there glided the shining thoroughfare of the tidal Thames, along which James the Second had fled from his people and every other King and Queen of England had gone about some grim business or sparkling holiday. In a park beginning two hundred yards west of his door the earlier of these monarchs had pursued the stag across the marshy flats traversed, still longer ago, by every race that had successively conquered England, each picking its way, in turn, towards the great ford across Thames at the mouth of the Brent.

Here, for quite three months, my friend's fine sense of figurative smell found fodder sufficient to sustain it. Wherever he sniffed at first, there came in a fine smack of the storied, the immemorial. He walked in the great park where Beatrix Esmond had ridden a-hunting; he played a little golf in the grounds of the house to which Jeanie Deans had been brought to plead for Eifie; he reconnoitred Cambridge House, where Dr. Johnson had dined, and the houses on the top of the hill where Reynolds had painted and Sheridan had drunk. He made out the landing-place at which Lady Jane Grey had, perhaps, taken boat to go down to the Tower. He sat now and then at the spot from which he judged that Turner's great "Richmond Hill" had been painted; also his admirable "Mortlake." Then, somehow, he broke down. The nourishment must not have had the body and bouquet of the old Italian stuff. He threw up his lease and fled to Rome, where the old odorous civilisations lie buried in layers and the scents come not in single notes but in thronging chords.

And yet, when I last saw him there, he had not the look of one of the happy. Few aromatists have. They "never are, but always to be, blest." They hunt their chymic gold with hungry looks and sometimes with faintly petulant voices that raise tough questions in plodding minds like yours and mine.

V

Is it, then, impracticable to live, not by bread alone, but wholly on cake? Was Charles the Ninth—or was it some other Charles?—right when he said that Florence was too lovely to look at except on a holiday? If ourselves could go and do as the aromatists, and did it for the rest of our days, should we feel, when we were dying, that we had been a kind of sneaks to keep our fingers so handy to all the nicest jam-pots all those years? Or should we feel that we had fought a sort of good fight and carried the banner of one sort of perfection, and that the kind most in danger of extinction in these slump years, as we are told that they are, for most of the things of the spirit? Certainly it were, as Trinculo says of mislaying the bottle, not only dishonour but infinite loss if the whole race of passionate practitioners of absorption in the savours of art and the atmospheres of history were to perish from the earth. But what about these particular ones, these perfectly-got-up but absolutely non-toiling and non-spinning lilies of the aesthetic field? What about their economic basis? Unless, of course, we count their informative conversation as an adequate output of commodities? No getting away from the fact that to keep these exquisites going, a certain number of other heirs of all the ages have to cramp their backs in mines or repeat uninspiriting manual movements in factories, under more or less pressure of pernicious gases. Gravely I fear that a Soviet Power might put its aromatists down for the very lowest scale of rations, along with the nobles and the divines. Or would some sagacious Soviet of the future preserve a few of them alive and functioning in cages, surrounded by stimulating objets d'art and models of extinct capitalistic buildings like the Bargello, Theodoric's Tomb, and the Palace of the Doges? Thus confined, they could at any rate do very little harm; like the beasts at the Zoo, they could be put to some educational use in teaching the sons and daughters of the proletariat about the dreadful philosophy of Epicurus.

Or is it that, economics apart, they have made a mistake, from which most of us have been saved, not wholly by ourselves? For most of us have the good luck to be at any rate reasonably poor. We have a living to get and cannot come and go as we like. If all our time were our own, nothing, perhaps, might preserve us from courting certain failure in life by the vulgar tactics of grabbing directly at joy instead of trying for something else and trusting joy to come in by the way while the trying goes on, or while we take breath between one mighty try and another. Because some spirit of delight had never failed our one short annual month of holiday rambling or scrambling in Italy or the Alps, we might fondly suppose that, by knocking off work altogether and keeping strictly to play, twelve times as large a portion of joy could be netted in one whole year. No doubt we should lay out vast plans: we should cast our nets wide. A winter in Egypt; an early spring among the bursting violets of Grasse; May and June in the tender Venetian foot-hills of the Alps; a midsummer feast of gentians and snow; and then an Elysian autumn with glowing Vallombrosan leaves and with art's co-extensive palette in the Uffizi and Pitti below. Ten to one, the plan would fail. Before we had done with the Nile we should probably find that the supply of magic light, which had never failed us before, had been firmly turned off at the main. For joy will not have herself ordered about like mutton or coal, of which any rich person can get as much as he chooses to pay for: she shies away from blunt or importunate wooing. All the "beauty spots" of Europe have always been haunted by the dull faces of rich suitors who have estranged her. You meet them in every hotel that guide-books term "first-class"; the plaint they make aloud is commonly about the food, but what they really mean is that streams have run dry in themselves and the choric spheres have got out of tune.

Joy will have flown off, the while, to where some one has got his head so well down to some commonplace job that he does not feel the time going—or else does feel it going, remarkably slowly, and still sticks to the job. There she hangs about, unseen and unthought of, plotting for liftings of mystical veils and revelations of well-springs for the benefit of this inconsiderable person. And presently, perhaps after much agonising study of his pass-book and of manuals of tariffs in hotels, the unsuspecting beneficiary ventures to take a short foreign holiday and finds that on some morning of sun after frost on a Chamonix peak he has seen the world in its making, or that when looking at some old picture in a Tuscan church he has observed the heavens opened and angels ascending and descending.

Yet whole-hog aromatists, people who flee their own country for good and live out the rest of their lives in Tuscan villas or somewhere near the Rialto, are often presentable men, well-taught and virtuous and communicable. When I was a 'prentice critic and used to damn middling plays that provoked the airy intolerance of my youth, a venerable friend would upbraid me with dissuading the public from the innocent exercise of uncritical play going. "After all, these people," he would say, with a wave of his hand towards the long-suffering denizens of the pit—"these people might have been in public-houses now." And so they might. And aromatists might have been fostering passions for cocaine. So let them by all means abide as they are. "God made them; therefore let them pass for men," as Beatrice said of another Italianate Englishman.

CHAPTER VII

FREE TO THE UTTERMOST

Whose service is perfect freedom.
Book of Common Prayer.

I

In travel it is good to be the master of your fate and to choose your destination and route. And yet in this as in other things there is one glory of the sun and another glory of the moon, a time to take charge and a time to refrain from taking it. It used to seem good fun to engage another child to tie a handkerchief round your eyes and lead you about blindfold, with many twists and changes of direction, stopping now and then to untie you and let you enjoy the choice sensation of seeing what strange and unexpected places you had reached. There is a queer luxury in it—akin, I suppose, to that other queer transport of ease that some of us get when we sit back, with even our heads held up in the right place, in the chair at the dentist's, to let him do what he will. All the rest of your time you are deciding and acting, perhaps for other people, controlling and judging and planning; at any rate you are commanding that turbulent unit, yourself. But now, for the hour at least, responsibilities are over. That curious joy, I suppose, is akin to the high and dangerous virtue of obedience as practised, in a kind of passionate trance of self-deposition, by some devout souls.

II

Almost the only adults, except some invalids, to whom travel of this voluptuous sort is likely to come are private soldiers. Officers know too much; the handkerchief is not properly over their eyes. Only to the doors of private soldiers, in war-time, does the real magic carpet come with sealed orders to carry them Heaven knows whither—to any part of any continent of them all. Many hundreds of thousands of men now alive must remember the charm of such voyaging, even in Europe. Some autumn day, perhaps, the bugles would blow them out of their sleep at three in the morning before a crimson sunrise had broken over Salisbury Plain. Everything would have changed in the night; there would be "harps in the air"; you would feel as you do at the times when you consciously slough some old manner of life, or a stage of your youth, like a skin; the good old camp would be looking already like some house to let, that once you had lived in. Then the minutes began to slip past with an odd, flowing swiftness, just as they do when you are being married or making a short speech that you have learnt well by heart, the sliding wheels of time seeming no longer to bite on your mind, but just to skid on and on. Soon you were gazing in a luxurious reverie out of a train already gliding down some meadowy valley. The Itchen could that river be? Circumstances undetermined by yourself surrounded the train—they even seemed at times to have some relation to you and your work: women stood at cottage doors shading their eyes and waving the other hand; shouts from little boys at level crossings shrilled suddenly up into hearing and dropped down behind, till the slowing train ran level across the wind-swept streets of a port and clanked and jolted over many sets of points to reach a quay with the famed Mauretania moored to it, flags flapping and cordage whipping and whistling blithely. Brine in the air, sunshine and wind on the face, and the heart astir with the strangeness of riding abroad into a wider world upon a reinless horse, with great things awaiting you everywhere, everywhere.

And then foreign travel, right on from the first bump and backward flinch of the ship from the baulks of a quay under the big reddish bluff that stands sentry to Havre—yes, you think you know Havre by that and the look of all the lines of railway sunk flush with the stone surface of the wharf. Perhaps you marched through haggard morning twilight, with powdery snow muting already the tramp of the men, to entrain at a goods yard cast away in a quarter such as goods yards inhabit. You climbed from the ground level into closed trucks. Thirty men to a truck, every truck a complete wooden box, with a few bits of straw and dry snowflakes stirring uneasily over its much chipped and dinted floor. You sat or lay in darkness, closing every chink in the wheeled box lest more flakes of snow should join the little dry eddying dance of dust that tried to begin on any square foot of unoccupied floor. From far ahead a crescendo clanging of couplings came back till it jerked your truck into motion. Hour after hour that train would bump and rumble along, with pauses and checks without number. It swerved into grassy sidings where boughs brushed its sides, and waited there so long that it seemed to have retired wholly from the world, while more eager trains would overtake and outstrip it, like the Roman legions thundering past the dreaming East. You might open a chink and look out and see nothing but grey opaque air speckled, close to your eyes, with falling white spots. Or a little clearance might come and show you whether you were still among the Norman orchards or had reached the blown sand-dunes along the northern coast, or had struck inland among the low, rumpled Picardy hills.

If you had travelled at all in northern France before the war, these occasional glimpses, which seldom showed you the name of a station, amused and excited you curiously. Some biggish town would loom up in twilight, with several churches sticking up out of it. Was it Amiens? You searched for the slim toy spire of wood, like a dart, glued on to a mighty stone plinth. No. Then Abbeville perhaps? Or St. Omer, sombre, enigmatical, Jesuit, with its three mighty church towers thrust up at the sky, one dark and two spectrally white, dominating the black mass of houses mediævally crowded below? Or St. Riquier, perhaps, of the glorious facade? Or Bethune, with the great buttress tower?

I remember a night of such travel, when snow had fallen all day and then left a clear sky, full of stars burnished with frost. Every one else in the truck was curled up in sleep on the floor, but it seemed waste to sleep while such things could be seen. Would life ever bring them again? I opened a shutter a couple of inches and saw a wild shining white world all be-jewelled with glints of light from a sky inlaid with flashing brilliants. Heaven knows where we were. I thought I saw osiers and watercress growing in linked chains of lagoons near a river. That looked like the Somme. And then rows of poplars, miles long, standing above a canal; and that also looked like the Somme. But then the ground crumpled itself into folds, and high on one side a great road was marching along the crest of a down, with all its roadside trees blown one way—all their lives, probably—so that, even on this frozen windless night, they looked like banners carried high in procession against a strong wind. Might that be the famous highway from Arras through St. Pol and Hesdin, the way that Spain's flooding power had rolled out westward from Holland and then drawn back in ebb? But soon the sky-line fell, the roads, half masked with snow, grew twisty without any visible reason; they serpentined over dead flats sharply lined with the snowless black streaks of ditches, where the hedges would have been in England. The way to Ypres? Heaven knew. I searched for the Great Bear and took the pointer to the Pole. Right over our engine the Pole-star was flashing. At times the train would yaw away to the right. It seemed to have found the turning, the place whence to go east and drop us into our unknown predestined slot—Arras, Loos, Kemmel, Armentieres, wherever our own fighting might have to be done. And then it would bend north again, like a compass needle, with random oscillations and yet with that wavering constancy to the Pole.

It engendered a strange exaltation. Forces outside us and now beyond our control, forces to which we had given ourselves in unreserved faith, had taken us up and were bearing us on as mothers carry their infants. And now I was alone in that world: sleep had for the moment dispeopled it. All the common look of the earth's surface had turned to white blankness almost as featureless as mist-filled air looked down upon from clear air above. With all these starry gauges of infinite space filling the upper concave hemisphere of the universe, and their reflected gleams lending a visionary lustre almost as unearthlike to the mirroring surface of the earth, imagination needed no forcing; there came spontaneously the sensation of being sped through interstellar space by some omnipotent force on some inscrutable errand to some destination unimaginable as yet, oneself knowing nothing, controlling nothing, only feeling an immeasurably deep repose of self-committal. Whatever might come was all right; wherever one went was the best place and the centre of the world. It was luxurious. I suppose that it must be a hunger for some higher form of this peace which passes all understanding that sends men and women trooping into the churches which offer to supply it in its greatest intensity. "In His will is our peace"; "Lead Thou me on; I do not ask to see"; "I loved to choose and see my path; but now Lead Thou me on." Raptures of self-submission like these may be virtue and holiness. Certainly they are pleasure— dangerous, perhaps, as most pleasures unluckily are, but exquisite.

III

An English soldier whose fortunes, for most of the war, were not out of the common, left England and landed in France by the same ports as Falstaff and Henry V. on their journey to Agincourt. He disembarked on the quay where Burne-Jones and Morris, walking there in their youth, had vowed themselves to the careers by which they were to tint the mind of educated England for a generation. He first marched up into the line across the country of Dumas' Three Musketeers, passing the belfry of Bethune and tramping the road to Cambrin which the son of Athos had ridden to join the Staff of Condd. Dulled for a time by the effects of combustion, his hunger for seeing the sights revived in a tent in the park of Versailles, near the Petit Trianon, where countless bunches of mistletoe sat still, like pheasants, on the boughs of trees that had been young with Marie Antoinette. When convalescent, he sojourned under canvas for two winter months upon the sands where Napoleon had mustered his grand armada of flat-bottomed craft for the projected descent upon England. Restored for a season to his own friends in the line, he was presently sent travelling again, this time by trench fever. He came to his wits, warm and at rest, in a marvellous tent lined with silk and double-walled, the gift of an Indian prince to an Emperor. Beneficent and inscrutable powers bore him away to a regal city where Joan of Arc had been burnt and King John had murdered Prince Arthur. When he could walk on a deck, genies carried him down to a quay and put him on board a black ship, to glide for a whole sunny April day down the unwinding coils of a river so divinely puissant and so fringed with divers delights to the eye, that a lifetime's loyalty to our queenly Thames was for some dizzy moments seriously imperilled. Falling early to sleep, the serene infant sleep of health reborn, he awoke to the sound of water lapping quietly under opened portholes— Southampton. Water rippling and shining, fringed with inviolate trees, the unshelled houses gleaming white and red among them: England ten times herself, intoxicatingly un-foreign. And the English trains, smooth movers along well-weeded tracks through cuttings vivacious with the English primrose, to drop the impersonally conducted tourist in a new dwelling-place of wonder, with Plymouth Sound below his window and Drake's bowling-green above his chimneys.

To charm him next there came a month of guarding on the Firth of Forth, of living in a half-dismantled ancient fort, a fort of Walter Scott, with Edinburgh Castle lifting to the skies above the great smoke in the south, and the first Highland hills to the north-west stretched out pensive in the long midsummer sunsets that always had the gaunt queer lines of the Forth Bridge laid down on them monstrously black; and once the great fleet streaming out in slow procession from its guarded haunt above the bridge, and returning a day or two later, diminished and bringing its wounded, some ships in tow, some with their funnels knocked awry, and moving slowly, as with pain; some with a first-aid dressing of red-painted bedding stuffed into holes in their sides; and then the first leave men coming chuckling ashore at the pier and telling the soldiers off duty how they had knocked Fritz at Jutland; their voices are audible still, and the laughter mingling in the summer night with a plashing of oars and elvish summer lightning while the sentry searchlight, grave, alert and steady on its post, wheels to and fro across the gateway of the Firth.

The spectacle of many battles followed—defeat and victory, always in illustrious places; the Somme with its sultry months of slaughter-house smell and flies and frustration; Arras, petering out in futile attrition after its first wondrous morning of tempest, rain and wasted valour, when the battle, seen from above, wrote itself clear in legible letters of flame on the blackboard of a moonless last hour of night; Messines, where all the British mines, exploding together in the fight's first moment, shook the little hill from which our soldier looked down upon the fight as if it were a little boat on a choppy sea; and Flanders, Cambrai, St. Quentin and all the great days of the three months of triumph.

Each had its own face and voice; in memory it is un-confusable with the rest. But they never were merely world-shaking events. Whatever they might be besides, they were always occasions of travel. They all beckoned the soldier to storied, illustrious places not chosen by him. His work would take him up to-day to the Vimy Ridge, our latest capture, to look across the central plain of the Low Countries, Europe's everlasting cockpit, the basin of the sluggish Scheldt, its flats diversified with Oudenarde and Ramillies, Jemappes and Quatre Bras and Waterloo.

To-morrow it would show him wild boars with their families, trotting down glades of the forest of Crecy. For some nights it sent him to sleep in the French country-house that has the field of Agincourt outside the paling of its park. It brought him into Miraumont, upon the Ancre, when German guns were knocking to pieces the last of all the pleasant ancient houses of that place, perhaps the very house in which the wild English prince, turned into a steady and a crafty king, slept on his way along our future Somme front of 1916 on his way to his own battle.

In his hours of ease the soldier was at liberty to sit with Quentin Durward on the topmost parapet of the tempestuous-historied Castle of Peronne. He saw black crowds of the women of two nations, a friend and an enemy, praying in bereavement and bitterness of soul in the cathedrals of Amiens and Cologne. To make a trinket for his wife he collected many coloured bits of ancient glass shattered or shaken by gunfire out of the glowing church windows of Ypres and Arras, St. Quentin and Liege. He lived in the places where Bardolph stole the pyx and where Richelieu put up when he rushed out from seventeenth-century Paris to pray to the French troops to head back the Germans—almost precisely where these were again headed back in 1918. The Belfry of Bruges gave his G.H.Q. car a night's shelter; he saw the German snipers slowly falling back before the English from street to street of the birthplace of Froissart; one day he passed Robespierre's birthplace in Arras, and that night he slept at an Artois chateau where some of the family portraits had notes to them saying that this bewigged Count was guillotined at Arras in the Terror, and that blonde Marquise died there in prison. Checked on the outskirts of Mons, on the war's last morning, by a new crater blown in the road, he found that he was in Malplaquet village; and, hurrying on to Brussels on some errand when fire had ceased, he crossed the field of Waterloo in a fog through which there appeared a troop of French Canadian horse trotting eastward, men of Napoleon's race, but fellow-citizens of Wellington, pressing on to the Rhine to occupy parts of the country of Bliicher. Everywhere history, legend, tradition, and he, the witness of it all, transported, without effort or choice, from one old cynosure of the world's eyes to another and another.

IV

Perhaps the effect of sealed orders upon the mind which receives them was strongest of all when the soldier moved alone, and not as an atom in the bulk of a moved battalion. To one who had known only the regimental life of a front there might come, as from a cloud or a burning bush, the sudden order to come to London, to put on officer's clothes and "stand by," prepared to "proceed overseas." You might be ordered to proceed, for all that you knew, to any of the continents, any lost end of the earth. And then the orders would come, like the instructions in fairy stories; the princes are bidden to go to some lonely place where a stranger charged with further directions shall meet them and know them by the exchange of a sign. From a certain station in London you were to take a certain train on a certain day. That was all. The train passed you on to a ship, majestically guarded by airship and destroyer; the ship put you out on a French quay and behold! an officer with a megaphone stood on the quay-side and composedly whooped to you directions to report at a neighbouring hut for orders. The power in the hut said "G.H.Q." and gave you a slip of buff paper containing the number of a car. The car awaited you upon the quay. Beside the bonnet the slave of the lamp stood expectant; he grasped and stowed your kit and jumped to the starter.

And now the charm began to work with all its power, in the case that I know best. It was late on a cloudless evening, the sun just going to set, a week or two after Midsummer Day. The car was a beauty, full of life and eagerness, and driven with spirit; it rushed at the hills like a horse going home. Before the sun was gone we had cleared the rout in the streets of Boulogne and climbed the crack that leads the road south-eastward up the coastal cliff of chalk and on to the rolling downs. Where G.H.Q. might be, I knew not. Of course I could have asked the driver, but—somehow, I did not want to know. At any rate, not yet.

The top of a down always gives a lift to your spirits. Its wide convexity feels as if it must be the spherical swell of the whole globe. Poised high on the great ball, you seem to look commandingly down on all its gently rounded slopes. Up and down the little undulations of the road the car sped joyously. It almost seemed to leave the earth for the air as it rushed the crest of each little rise.

A village on a beacon height looked quaintly gay as we passed through; the first lights were just coming out blithely in houses that stuck on like swallows' nests under the eaves of the church: then down a big dip and up again on to the crown of the downs, the place of high spirits. I looked back from the top and the sun was gone now, leaving the north-western sky aglow with solemn bars of russet flame; the nearer trees stood, flat as black lace laid on a crimson dress, against that subsident pomp; ahead the woods were darkening on the low ridges. The bloom was on the hour; the visible world, that shifts and changes and re-makes itself as ceaselessly as a blown flame, had caught for a moment the fugitive poise of perfection that seems almost passionate, making the senses ache with a delight that is also a longing to transcend one's own commonness and to shape new, clearer thoughts. Luxuriously I put off asking whither we were going. Enough to be projected out into the summer night and the unknown. The eager wheels licked up the road, the unfamiliar villages slid past, a voluminous river seemed to be bearing me chartless, rudderless and anchorless, bound to whatever might come and yet, in spirit, almost ecstatically free.

To sleep I give my powers away;
My will is bondsman to the dark;

I sit within a helmless bark.

What waking freedom is like that freedom of reverie? "Like them that dream"—the words were well chosen to figure the joy of Zion delivered from captivity. Somewhere far off in the gathering dark strange hands, perhaps, were making a bed and cooking food; some unknown brain was easing me of man's besetting worry of finding the right thing to do and the right place to make for; a world that looked like an absolute master was really my servant—at every new turn it would take the labours of decision off my hands and bear for me all the distresses of perplexity. "I am the clay and thou art the potter"—what an exultant cry of emancipation it is! To take right shape, to serve fine ends, and all without struggle, or choice, but in trances of utter open-armed surrender to something you take, once for all, to be better than you.

"G.H.Q., sir! Montreal!" My driver broke in on my musings. We had just topped the crest of a ridge: he pointed across a deep valley in front, to a little hill heavily wooded and darkling now in the thickened dusk. Among the softer curves of foliage a few slightly harder lines of ancient fortification could just be made out. The car flew silent down a long hill and crossed a marshy bottom to address itself to the steep winding road of access to a tiny walled city set upon that small wooded hill. In two minutes more a sentry had halted us under a massy brick arch that was built by Vauban. Where Sterne had had his papers checked, upon his Sentimental Journey, the English corporal of the guard looked carefully by lantern light at mine and then, falling back to attention, saluted and passed me on into the little dark streets where Chaucer had walked as an English envoy and Ney had commanded the left of Napoleon's army that was to cross over and subjugate England.

CHAPTER VIII

LITTLE ENGLAND

Love comes in at the eye.
W. B. YEATS.

I

What sort of love could a mother expect from a son who had never yet got a good sight of her face, although he had seen, shall we say, the tips of a few of her nails, or perhaps a square inch of her skin?

Of course he might well have heard many fine things about her. He might be proud of her fame and the stir that she had made in the world; grateful, too, for what she had done for himself. But this is not love. As with your mother, so with your country. An Englishman who has never seen England full face may certainly find much about her for gratitude, goodwill and pride to linger upon. At sight of all the red paint on a map of the world he may find an agreeable sense of property warming him. Truly a large and a handsome estate! Or, again, the mixture of Celtic, Teutonic and other serviceable elements in English blood may gratify his common sense. Or his mind, with its fine political instincts, may run complacently upon such topics as freedom slowly broadening down from precedent to precedent. Or he may be uplifted in heart on reflecting how many more millions of Mahometans he and his brethren control than even the regular Commander of the Faithful. And yet, strictly speaking, none of these pleasant emotions is love, either.

Tell me, where is fancy bred?
How begot, how nourished?
It is engendered in the eyes,
By gazing fed. . . .

Love might well come in at the eyes of the first Romans of all. On the mound where the Capitol was to be, they could stand and survey the whole of the cramped village below and the crush in the tiny Forum. They saw, without having to turn their heads round, their whole motherland. And love may well have come easy for some early Venetian sailor homing across the Adriatic at night and espying through the dark the little groups of lights shining out from the wonderful camp that he and his comrades in trouble had pitched on the face of the sea. The sons of Monaco, again, when not busy filling the hungry with good things and sending the rich empty away, may obtain ardent filial emotions to-day when they walk up to Turbia, look down and view at one glance the whole land of their birth basking and shining, compact in the sunshine below. But what is to happen when no single gaze can take in the whole of the object of which it is meet that we be enamoured?

No one, said Fox, could really be in love with Mrs. Siddons. Her scale, the huge structure of her genius, precluded any tender approach. In the court of love, as humanity knows it, her head would be sticking out through the roof. You might as well cherish a passion for Ursa Major or for the East India Company. And modern man, presented with an Empire or a continent for a mother, may seem like some good little fellow of middling intelligence given in wedlock to a Tragic Muse. "I have already," a troubled American said when the Philippines were delivered into his hands, "more country than I can love." In the writings of Mr. Kipling the most piercing cry of patriotic longing is no fine flourish about lordship over palm and pine, but the wail of the Cockney soldier in India for London, "the sounds of 'er and the sights of 'er" and the smell of the orange-peel, asphalte and gas. There is, as every one knows, a patriotism that calls out for size, always more size. "Das Vaterland muss grosser sein," a German patriotic chorus used to say, and a popular hymn to England said ditto:

Broader still, and broader
Shall thy bounds be set;
God, who made thee mighty,
Make thee mightier yet.

But the love which is wholly love clings instinctively to things that are within the reach of sense, and small enough to be held in one grasp. It cannot embrace abstract nouns nor the glories of conscious extensiveness. Indeed, it may suffer pangs of the haunting apprehension of mothers. "Some day," they say to themselves, as they look at the child on their knees, "he will be too big to lie in my lap any more."

II

From Leith Hill, in Surrey, the Shoreham gap in the South Downs allows you to see the shining waters of the English Channel. Then, if you turn to the north, you may see, when London's smoke does not hide it, the low line of south Middlesex hills about Highgate. From Highgate Hill to Finchley is only an afternoon's walk, and from Finchley to Barnet is nothing: each of these is within easy view of the next. From Barnet Hill, again, Ridge Hill is well within sight, and from Ridge Hill you see in fair weather the Minister church of St. Albans. Northward St. Albans looks up to the white Chiltern wall, and on gaining the crest of that wall, by the Holyhead road, you see across the valley of the Ouse the low sky-line of the Cotswolds trailing away into the north-east. On days when the air has been well washed with rain you may just descry from a well-picked point on the top of the Cotswolds the darkling bulge of the Peak. The Peak looks westward on Snowdon, and winter climbers on Scawfell have seen the streaks of snow that mark the northern gullies of the Carnedds, Snowdon's neighbours across the Holyhead road. Scawfell is a morning's walk from Skiddaw, and from Skiddaw the Cheviots are easily seen. The Cheviots look on the Lammermuir Hills, the Lammermuir Hills on Arthur's Seat, and if you sit on Arthur's seat and look north, across the Forth, on any fine day, the Highland mountains form your horizon.

Get to know by heart the view, forward and back, from each link of this chain of dominant heights. Then stand at one of them, close your eyes, and call up, with all the force of your imagination, what you would see from each of the others. If you are well stirred by the joy of the game, you may find that the several clear pictures are fusing into one picture, scarcely less clear, of the whole length of the island. At last you have succeeded. You have rendered all England impossibly and beautifully small. You may have made her almost as practicable an object of sense, and of sensuous love, as some garden in which you played as a boy.

Think what impression you get if you go by express train from London to Durham or Carlisle. Unless you have taken topography for a hobby, you probably see little more than a succession of fields so long that you cannot remember how many fields there were, nor their shapes, nor their order. They are. to you, countless; the country composed of them figures before your mind as something undelimited and so, in a sense, limitless or infinite—the sense in which Greek philosophy used the word infinite, meaning chaotic or formless, in contrast with the quality of things which art had made to certain chosen dimensions and proportions, or science had brought within the bounds of definition and comprehension. To convert that infinitude of passing fragments of scenery into something finite and coherent is to learn how to travel.

There are not, after all, so very many fields along the railway from King's Cross to Durham, or from Euston to Carlisle. A boy who daily goes ten miles to school by train soon knows by heart every field that he passes, and how each is hedged off from the next. Each field will fall easily into its place as soon as your eye and your topographic imagination have got well to work, in collusion, upon the main visible facts of England's structure. Then the entire country starts shrinking; the whole of its modelling comes into sight of your mind, endued with the fascinating minuteness and saliency of a model; its make, the lie of the rocks, sands and clays in which its relief is worked out, emerges curiously various within a tiny compass, like some Lilliputian plan of a large, diverse country. Soon some familiar marks on your motherland's surface do really become, and not in rhetoric only, like traits in the face of a human mother; the three crooked bars of slightly raised ground that traverse the mid-England plain from south-west to north-east are like remembered lines on her face; and the thought, in absence, of the coloured strips of soil, whitish, russet and brown, that run the same way, may begin to have power to move you like a recollection of her hair and eyes.

All authentic affection rests upon vision. Vision, again, rests upon knowledge. But minerals will not turn into flesh without first turning into something vegetable: so a mere intellectual grasp of a country's physique will not, alone, engender love of it. Knowledge has first to pass into vision, the state of mind and heart which does not merely apprehend evidence but broods excitedly over some completed and transfigured image of an apprehended object. Once attain that condition, once make knowledge sensuous, and then none of nature's limitations on the ordinary reach of the senses need disable you. England, bewitchingly small, lies complete at your feet; she rides like a boat at her moorings, off Europe;

all of her nestles below you like Macclesfield seen from the moors, or Florence from Fiesole. Then the grand passion may come, the love that can revel and dote on the very idea of the beloved. But vision comes first; the lover must see the beloved and not merely have read her biography, very well done, and a scientific account of her person.

III

Unless you go wrong in some way, and get out of your place, you are sitting, all your days, at the centre or hub of several successive rings or concentric zones of demand upon your natural affection. Smallest and nearest and pressing in around you everywhere comes the exigent call of your family. Next beyond it, the call of your country. Then the call, it may be, of some fraternity of comrade countries, of which your own is a member—the British Empire, perhaps, or a league of Latin-American States. Lastly, the outermost circle of all, the call of human brotherhood.

Many well-meaning persons would set these affections on by the ears, to worry and bite one another. Some cry down all national patriotism as a bane to pure love of mankind; others sneer at mere depth of affection for "Little England" as if it must needs be something taken away from your fund of proper regard for Madras and Hong Kong; Plato and others have had a spite at the family's calls on the heart, and many good souls bear a grudge to general human comradeship; they do not like to hear it mentioned, lest a goodwill that comprehends aliens should weaken the mutual kindness that binds up a tribe.

Of course it is true that any one of these affections may suffer perversion and prove once again that a good thing gone bad may stink like the worst. Nations have undergone torments because a King wanted, at any cost, to be nice to his new wife, or because a mother could not bring herself to think of anything but getting or keeping a throne for her son. Quite fervent lovers of man as a whole have been known to abandon their wives or neglect their infants or let their country go hang. And patriotism has served, at different times, as widely different ends as a razor, which ought to be used to keep your face clean and yet may be used to cut your own throat or that of some more innocent person. Charity, as Bacon says, will scarcely water the ground if she must first fill a pool; from any one of these concentric circles of appeal to your affection there may come a kind of vampire shriek that will derange and disable you past all power of making a decent response to the other appeals as well as to itself. Nepotism has ravaged public and private affairs, mothers have ruined children with petting and Bishops have given excessive preferment to curates of poor quality who had married the Bishops' daughters; warm love of humanity in the abstract has served as a specious excuse for the cold shoulder turned to concrete specimens of the breed or to those beautiful little groupings of local comrades, called nations; men and women have got as disgustingly drunk on patriotism as on wine. Yet wine, although Iago said it, "is a good familiar creature, if it be well used." And so is patriotism. So are all these various movings of human tenderness. All that is wrong with any of them is also wrong with almost every splendid thing that we have: it is dogged by a kind of base shadow, misshapen and dark. As passion is shadowed by sentimentality, holiness by cant, originality by eccentricity, and eloquence by rhetoric, each of these wholesome emotions is followed about by some weak and extravagant double or travesty of itself, a kind of idiot cousin full of sound and fury, signifying nothing, or possibly full of imbecile cunning. Yet the authentic feeling, in every case, is as sound a provision of nature as each of that other set of concentric circles you see in the cut trunk of a tree. Both sets have grown sanely aright and express in the clearness and strength of all their widening rings a natural operation of years and of unmarred health.

All of them natural, still these concentric affections cannot all be alike. The nearest circular ripples sent out by a stone thrown into water cannot resemble exactly the more distant circles of undulation that follow. The outer ripples have to forgo something of depth in return for their ampler circumference. And love pumped outwards around us by engines so small as our own hearts must also lay its account with physical limits and laws. As all love rests, at last, upon impressions got with the bodily senses, and these are compelled to abide by some pretty hard terms as to reach and power of penetration, the basis of each of these zones of affection is qualified in a way of its own. Love of parents and children has endless gazing to feed on. Love of country is less richly fed, though most of us have formed some dim sensuous impression, at least, of the look of the hedged English fields, the dews and gentle warmth of English summers, or the line of undulation in English voices. Love of a world-wide Empire lives on such scraps as it can find; a traveller whose ship reaches by night some tropical quay may hear, with a sudden surge of joy, the accent and idiom of London emerging from backgrounds of palm and bamboo; for those who cannot travel the diet is meagre; the senses have to pick up such crumbs as travelling writers and artists contrive to let fall from their tables. Love of all humanity, less richly fed again, has to become still more an affair of inference, indirect fire, or distillation, always in danger of lapsing down to the merely intellectual plane and becoming only a matter of thoughts worked up about thoughts, all unlit and un-warmed by any sensuous vision.

It seems as if the heart, aware of this descending scale of closeness of sensuous contact with natural objects for its affection, instinctively tried to contract or compress each circle towards the more caressable smallness of the circles within it. Such phrases as "the human family," "the British family of nations," and, less directly, "greater Britain" indicate the working of that inclination. Most strongly of all does it animate the impulse to put one's own country, in imagination, under a kind of inverted microscope, to think it down and down, smaller and smaller, into complete simultaneous visibility. Love, indeed, of every kind has an inveterate habit of painting in miniature. The language of lovers has always been quite a glossary of diminutives. Falstaff himself is Doll's "sweet little rogue." The noblest of all patriotic descants upon England is also the veriest cataract of these terms of endearment. Old Gaunt's famous tirade is composed of delighted assertions that England is small, very small. She is a "little" world, a snug fortress, a mere garden "plot," a moated house, a tiny jewel in a wide silver setting of sea. "The fatherland must greater be," says the common politician, always concerned for growth and expansion. "God, who made thee little, make thee lesser yet," is the half-conscious prayer of the absolute lover, to whom his mistress never appears as a creature that needs extension or improvement, but always as an accomplished perfection; all he craves is that this best of good things should never pass beyond the compass of his embrace.

In some of these great lovers you may even find a trace of lurking jealousy of the wide power and fame of the beloved. Desiring that all English people should feel as they themselves do, they are dimly uneasy lest the British Empire be a dangerous rival to England for Englishmen's love. Some of them brood on the malady of ancient Rome, whose extremities throve at the cost of her heart. They wonder, can we still be breeding in our shires rustics of the racy pith and vehemence and humour of the clowns whom Shakespeare manifestly knew? Or has the bursting sap of England's strength passed out into the ends of the earth to animate strange types of semi-English hardihood and wit, Australian, Canadian and what not? For hollyhocks bloom at their overgrown tips when autumn has stripped already the older part of their stems. Or they may have worried lest something most recognisably and endearingly English was fraying itself away out of existence, at least out of grasp, during the long revel of worldly success, supreme wealth and high consideration that ended with the war.

Hast thou yet dealt her, O life, thy full measure?

World, have thy children yet bowed at her knee?
Hast thou with myrde-leaf crowned her, O pleasure?
Crown, crown her quickly, and leave her to me.

Even short of these subtle aches and misgivings, the love of country that doeth and beareth all things must fear all things too. Wherever she goes, a lover's mind follows his mistress in absence, and sees the flat earth capable of rising up to strike her and mountains falling on her head. Fear is a realist painter, and these tremors help to keep her imperilled figure, as she walks, vivid to the mind—perhaps the turn of her head as she steps off a curb to cross the tangled currents of a city's traffic. So, where your love is the real thing, will your country be feared for and, when most feared for, most clearly and movingly seen, corporeal and personal with a personality almost more salient than life itself. Common man as you may be, insensibly you begin to trench on the privileges of the chartered poets. Before you know it you are personifying the England of your affectionate reveries. Say that you fear some mean thing may be done by politicians in her name—how easy then to feel that something alive, a figure in distress, is hanging its head or wandering restlessly in the twilight Chiltern beechwoods or by the silent head-waters of Isis or Avon. To Reason, with her austere ways, Reason who does not walk in the ways of her heart nor in the sight of her eyes, the thing that we had to fear in the autumn of 1914 was the loss of what power we had to live our own lives in the way that we chose, and to do this as of right and not by the leave of any one else. But you and I, whom blood warms, could not get out of sight of something less abstract and more of a person, near akin to us, some one inviolate still, but horribly threatened. It seemed to have taken almost physical shape out of that more nebulous vision we have of a country's spirit or soul, the indwelling product or sum of all the strong, kindly, courageous and wise actions ever done by any of its children. This had, of a sudden, acquired the compelling poignancy of things that appeal to the soul through the bodily senses; not any mere intellectual definition of England but Rotha and Wye themselves were alarmed and cried out for relief; even the autumn mists over flat lowland meadows, to which soldiers awoke in their camps, became movingly English; they looked almost precarious; they asked to be helped to go on, just as they were. You felt as the young feel when a mother, the most assured and immutable thing in their own past, has fallen dangerously ill; you gained that sudden revelation of the bravery and beauty that belong to any endangered life.

I suppose that gifted persons, Old Gaunts and the like, can summon these visions at will. Most of us they visit seldom; some, perhaps, never, or how could any such thing as a war-profiteer be? To fit ourselves to entertain them is all we can do—to keep the house clean and the guest-chamber garnished; and this above all—to know our country by sight, the kind of sight that overleaps the wall between bodily and imaginative sense and makes the operations of the two continuous, so that the sight puts itself forth with almost equal eagerness and success on what is literally present and on what is remembered.

CHAPTER IX

ALONG AN ENGLISH ROAD

... *as common as the way between Saint Albans and London.*
King Henry IV. Part II. II. ii.

I

To know a country it is not enough to have seen some tit-bit of a place here and there. What do they know of England who only know Chester and Stratford-on-Avon, Warwick and Winchester, Oxford and Windsor? The land is the common run of the land, both the choice and the poor, barren place and fertile; everything that Caliban showed Prospero—"all the qualities o' th' isle." And yet you must come to know them as things connected and truly parts of a whole. To this latter end there is no better means than to make friends with some one great trunk road. Get to know, for example, the road from London to Manchester, running through St. Albans, Woburn, Northampton, Leicester, Derby and Buxton. That done, your knowledge of England will have a backbone, something central, columnar and sturdy. Everything else that you come to know later will fall easily into its place as tissue attached to that spinal pillar.

What is it, though, that we mean here by "knowing" a road? Not just seeing it all once or twice from a seat in a car and having it on the word of your own eyes that the southern Midlands are mainly grass land and the Peak country rocky. Nor yet need you learn it by heart, to the last house and tree, as children learn the few hundred yards of road to and from school. There is a mean—to know it as people soon come to know the daily way home from a new place of work. Of that you make no set study; you do not cram it up; rather you leave your mind merely ajar, to let in such ideas of it as may come. Try, when you are not upon it, to call the course of it up, and it comes back less like a continuous line than a row of dots, bright beads strung thinly on a dim string. Not the road so much as points upon the road have taken the mind—here a fine or an ugly church, there a tree with odd boles or a name on a shop; yet, in a way, they are all joined; from each to the next your perception has moved as a climber on rock works from hold to hold, feeling back while reaching out, grasp passing into grasp, to be merged in the one act of adhesion made up of them all.

That is how to know a great road; you know it enough when you can shut your eyes, call up a row of points upon it, and feel how, as you went along, your senses only quitted their hold upon each when they had the next to fix on; how, say, as you set out from London for Manchester your eye travelled from Hampstead across the wide and deep dip to Finchley Church on its further bank, and then from Finchley over the next great trench to the knot of houses on the crest of High Barnet, and how from Barnet you traced the wooded line of Ridge Hill in the north-west, and, gaining Ridge Hill, just spied St. Albans Minster on the horizon, picked out by its harder lines from the softly modelled woods that it seems to spring from. So the grasp that your senses have of the road is carried on to the end in a kind of rhythm, as you go the length of a gymnasium through the air by a row of hanging rings, just carried by the end of each swing into reach of the ring that waits for you next, to hand you on in its turn. To leave no gap ringless in your memory, to be able in bed at night to go over it all, nowhere at a loss for the next hold—that will suffice. And all the better if the holds be well spaced out, so that the mind must reach out with a will and the eye learn to look at country in the large, till it can see, or almost see, the Vale of Trent as a whole, or the oneness of the crumpled and worn arch of red sandstone and coal, millstone grit and mountain limestone over which you can ride a push-bicycle in a short day between Stockport and Derby.

II

There was sense in that son of Jacob who "saw that rest was good," but also saw "the land, that it was pleasant." One evening, late in a very hot June, these two perceptions fell out with each other and argued, inside me. Bed was the place, said the former perception, after the toils of the day; it was bed, rightly used, that had made us the men that we are. Bed, the other perception replied, was *vieux jeu*;

bed could be had any night; base was the slave who went tamely to bed on the octave of Midsummer Night; this was the season for more intensely glowing delights; let me but mount my machine at midnight, in front of the Manchester Royal Exchange and, like Macbeth when he put his hand to a job, "ne'er shake hands nor bid farewell to it," except for the duration of reasonable meals, till I had crossed this green and pleasant land to Charing Cross; on the way I should see what I should see. A push-bicycle, I had felt, was the thing. You certainly see most when you walk, but you cannot walk to London in a day, and one unbroken day's view of the whole stretch of road was the object. By car the thing would be easy, but then travel by car is only semi-travel, verging on the demi-semi-travel that you get in trains. You must feel a road with your muscles, as well as see it, before even your eyes can get a full sense of it. So the active form of pleasure had it. By 1.40 A.M. the miles had begun to draw out between my forsaken pyjamas and me.

Of course a ride from Manchester to London within the twenty-four hours has no sort of rank as a physical feat. Any long-distance cyclist who counts would jeer at an average pace of ten miles to the hour for nineteen net hours of riding. "You loitered on the road too long," he would say, like the Rossettian princess's maid, rebuking the laggard in love. So let it be owned with adequate shame there were hours, a good two or three, during that Dog-day's torrid afternoon, when desire failed and the molehill was as a mountain, constancy an escutcheon, and pleasure herself, in the form that I had decided to woo, a cymbal tinkled out of tune; a time when the fairest of all Queen Eleanor's Crosses—it stands hard by the road, a little out of Northampton—could ravish the soul no more than an Albert Memorial; a time when the ante-meridian drift that had set towards London with the seeming passion of the Pontic current for the Hellespont was marvelously enfeebled and almost minded to compound— as if the Pontic current had dallied with the thought of going back to the Black Sea by train and letting the Mediterranean go hang. Nothing but wicked pride and such a high-tea as makes history—Newport Pagnell, in Bucks, was the theatre of this dispensation—decided the victory. Thenceforward brother body, to use the good Franciscan phrase, was visited by that irrational freshness which, if you have any luck, may come towards the end of a long day's good going. Lighting my lamp at St. Albans I slid down upon the capital in what may be called a state of repose, as compared with its arduous predecessors.

No sublime or momentous impression was achieved. Still, there remains in the memory something pleasant, a kind of ribbon-like frieze figured with successive images of divers ways in which man goeth forth to his labour, or cometh away from it, all round the clock, between a northern and a southern English midnight. In recollection, the frieze begins to march past like a film, beginning with lights in the windows of miners in Cheshire, south of Hazel Grove; then, in the first morning twilight, a gamekeeper, back from some nightly patrol, slips quietly in at the door of his cottage near Disley; soon the earliest reaping-machine is singing already, high up on a slope above Whaley Bridge; a couple of tramps show up black and enormous against the tepid, just-risen sun on the skyline of Taddington Moor, south of Buxton, their faces and hands, when seen nearer, blue with the coldness of all sleeping-out without blankets, even in summer; all down the Wye Valley the milk carts to go to the train stand by the cow-shed doors, staid and ready amid the vivacity of be-jewelled meadows and broken waters; at Rowsley the earliest dust of the day is stirred by the feet of day-shift men going in to the big Midland sidings; day and its work have undoubtedly come for the factory hands that flock in, as I pass, to the big mill at Cromford.

All this first lap of the frieze, the six-hour stretch before breakfast to Derby, has got an atmosphere of its own. Celestial light of the first quality apparels it. This is the tritest of observations. But all the best part of experience consists in discovering that perfectly trite pieces of observation are shiningly and exhilaratingly true. You find, in some fortunate state of yourself, that a fascinating innocence animates the long interval between the first peep of day on fine summer mornings and the hour for the general shifting of man from the horizontal to the vertical plane, although a thousand poets and prosers have already said so. The sleeping houses, with all their drawn blinds, do really, in spite of much ineffective literary certification of the fact, take on an ingenuous infantine air that is engaging and almost touching; the birds, after that first prelude which is so divertingly and humanly sleepy and nothing else, sing their jumbled matins as if they had really thought before dawn that this time the night might go on for ever and ever; the young rabbits and voles practise in these first ecstatic hours a happy boldness that seems to fail them before most of us are up; as I rode slowly up the long hill on the moors north of Buxton the capers cut in the white dust ahead by one furry prima ballerina and her offspring enlarged my conception of the dance as an expressive art.

Surely the young of man, too, ought to be much abroad at such hours.

My eight o'clock bacon and eggs at Derby drew a firm frontier between these auroral raptures and the dewless period which most of us call morning. Riding forth from Derby I breasted for some miles a powerful inward current of clerks. Outside this system of concentric suction the broad Vale of Trent was all in a hum. The air had been as quiet as a nun before; now the multifarious buzz of grasshoppers, flies, bees and the rest was swelling insistently up towards the dry roar of Dog-day noons. From each small town the rakish little carts of bare-headed butchers were radiating lightly on their quest for orders; young housewives, not without baskets, were closing behind them the garden gates of trim vi las and cycling away to the day's shopping in Shardlow or Loughborough. About Leicester the outward tide of butchers seemed to have paused, turned and set inwards. But I am not very sure. While morn had been losing its innocence, sense too, the wayfarer's enjoying retina, may have suffered some obscuration. All travel is pleasure, but this middle third of my journey must have been only pleasure, and not ecstasy, nor revelation, as travel should be. Else how should Market Harborough, attained at 12.30, be only embalmed grossly in memory now as the scene of a monumental repast, a shining masterpiece in beef and apple tart and beer, and of a smoke overshadowed by thoughts of its too early end? Perhaps, however, Northampton town at half-past three, when my brethren the tramps were all prone in Elysian siesta beside the white roads, throughout this broad land, was the place that brought the delighted spirit nearest to the status of a kneaded clod.

After the strong revivalist impulse at Newport Pagnell, at five, everything throve. Among the aromatic shadows of the Woburn woods I composed, about seven o'clock, a quarrel which I had for some hours been waging against the brutal white glare of the macadam dust, all un-tarred in that age, just ahead of the point where the front wheel laps up the road. With this hatchet decently buried, the life and labour of the English people became once more, in my sight, a cheerful and a changeful page. Lovers in pairs were soon coming out with the stars, and hay-carts piled up like cumulus clouds were lumbering home in the dark to Hertfordshire farms. A little south of St. Albans you pass into the suction system of London. Nearly all my fellow-cyclists now were Londoners, homing from some good evening's ride after work. Riding all day across England and passing town after town, each with its own daily rhythm of centripetal and centrifugal pulses, you are, in your small way, vbcvghbn like one of those light-rays of Einstein's that feel for a while, now and then, as they traverse the interstellar void, the loca pull of one wayside planet after another.

I crossed Mayfair at eleven. It sounded and looked as it commonly does on hot nights at that time of the year—many men in evening coats walking about from one house to another, keeping as cool as they could; a big hum, like that other one of the field insects, coming half-muted through open windows above; at other doors, footmen standing about in the cool bath-like dark, considering the f rmament on high or else the comedy below, in the grateful absence of their employers. Every one was quite good in his part. Every one had been, all day; yea, even at Northampton. But this kind of rush, though jolly once in a way, and liberal in impressions of its own, is only one of the lesser aids to intimacy with a road.

III

Overland travel is all, you may say, mountaineering. For no country is flat, not even Russia, not even Holland. Certainly some of the hills that diversify the whole earth are higher than others; those of the Lincolnshire fen-land are as much lower than the Alps as the Alps are lower than the Himalaya. Still, it is only a question of higher or lower relief; there is always relief. For any patch of land, a continent or an eyot, to keep above water, its surface has to be shaped more or less like the back of a hippopotamus or a whale, with a spinal ridge somewhere or other, highest of all, and all sorts of ribby ridges and inter-costal hollows dropping down from that spine to the water-line on each side. The sailors in Sinbad, who took the whale's back for an island, were not so far wrong, after all. Somehow or other, the water has to be made to run off the back of every emergent island or beast: everything has to be on a slope. From the summit ridge, wherever it be, lateral ridges must slope away to each side. From each lateral ridge, in its turn, minor ridges must slope away on each of its own flanks. And this diminuendo ridging must go on down to the modelling of every field by a brook, the earth as persistently seeking lower and lower levels as does the water that drops step by step from the tip of Mont Blanc or the Matterhorn down to the Adriatic.

So it comes that to go from any one point to another, in any country, is rather like one of the journeys made by a fly walking about on the back of a horse more or less bony. Perhaps the fly may only go over one rib into the valley between this and the next rib; or over several ribs; or it may walk straight across the backbone of the horse to a point on the other side; or it may make a vast oblique journey, starting, say, from between the two lowest ribs on the off side of the horse and ending at a point low down on its near shoulder. For this last purpose the fly's natural route would first be across rib after rib on the off side, always with an upward tendency towards the spinal ridge; then right over this eminence—the easiest route being between the two lowest vertebrae at its middle—and thence a downward and forward slant across one near rib after another.

All this time the fly would be mountaineering—always either dragging itself up a slant or letting itself down one. It would, with some differences in the degree and the nature of the relief, be doing just what a mountaineer does when he takes, say, the high-level route from Chamonix to Macugnaga. First, from his starting hollow between two northern ribs of the skeleton of Central Europe, the mountaineer would cross over some other ribs which also trend away to the north—he might cross the Verte or Dru rib by the Col des Grands Montets, the Chardonnet ridge by the Col du Chardonnet, the Corbassiere ridge by the Col des Maisons Blanches, and the Grand Tave ridge by the Col des Otanes. Then, seeing a good depression between the Mont Gele and the Mont Avril, two vertebrae in a kind of saddle-like depression in the spinal ridge of Central Europe, he might cross over the Col de Fenetre into the Valpelline dimple between two southern ribs, and thence eastward over one southern rib after another till Macugnaga was reached.

All inland travel is strictly like this of the mountaineer's or the pedestrian fly's. Especially so is travel by railways. For railways, with high costs of haulage to think of, follow with special care the practice of sage mountaineers. The sage mountaineer, with a new and difficult rock ridge to traverse, looks out for a good deep nick in its sky-line, and also for some scaleable-looking gully cut deep into the face of the ridge by the action of water. If such a gully, leading to such a nick in the main ridge, is visible, that is clearly his way—the easiest route to go and the least height to surmount. And this is, of course, the choice of the railway engineer, too. You may see it made over and over again as you travel by what used to be the Midland train from Manchester to London.

On this most beautiful and exciting journey the problem set to the train is almost precisely that which faces the fly on the horse's back, with its long oblique journey ahead, or the mountaineer starting from Chamonix for Macugnaga. At Manchester Central Station the train for St. Pancras starts pretty low down on the off side of the horse's back—supposing the horse to stand with his head to the south. The train is deep in the valley of the Mersey, between the lateral rib of high moorland that runs out westwards from the Pennine spine in the Bolton region and the similar westward rib that springs from the same spine near Buxton—the Cat and Fiddle rib you might call it. But, instead of crossing this next westward rib, the bold train makes straight for the spine itself, crosses it at the big tunnel beyond Chapel-en-le-Frith, and finds itself, near Peak Forest Station, looking down a relatively precipitous hillside—the upper part of the eastern slope of England. Before it, on its way to London, lies an oblique downward traverse of four near-side ribs, with London visible (to the passenger who has topographical vision) deep in the fifth hollow beyond the fourth intervening rib.

The first four intercostal hollows are the valleys of the Trent, the Welland, the Nen and the Ouse, all falling eastward towards the North Sea. The fifth is that of the Thames. And the train's first problem is one familiar to mountaineers who have reached the crest of an unexplored rock ridge which they desire to cross. How to get down to the bed of the valley below? The climber hunts about for a gully that seems to lead down without an absolute precipice to hold him up at any point in it. So does the St. Pancras train; it chooses the gully eaten out of the mountain limestone by the Wye, and down this fissure it cautiously lowers itself or glissades to the nearly flat floor of the wide Trent valley near Thrumpton. There the converse problem arises—how to get up the gradient between the Trent and Kibworth, where the topographic eye has already picked out a likely nick in the sky-line of the ridge forming the water-parting between Welland and Trent. Good mountaineering, again. The train selects the gully—a decidedly shallow gully, of course, but the principle is the same—of the Trent's big southern tributary, the Soar, just as a climber to the little col between Scawfell Pinnacle and the main mass of Scawfell may climb up beside the trickle of water that comes down Steep Ghyll. And so the four-hour climb goes on, ridge after ridge, till the chalk and the flints of the Chilterns have been surmounted, near Luton, and the train runs easily down the side of the wide clay-ware saucer in which London is laid.

IV

Surely, by this time, some one is saying: "O, but this is all platitude. This is all in the standard geography books." It is. It lies buried in them, dead as a doornail. You meet men and women, unfortunate souls, on whom that journey by train makes no impression but that of a great many fields, of all shapes and sizes, a few nameless rivers crossed here and there, and some picturesque scenery in the Peak. They may "know," in a sense, how their country is made, but the knowledge lies inanimate in their minds. Such knowledge has to be raised from the dead, as by miracle; dry bones have, by some magical touch, to be made to give praise; natural facts which are certified real in books but have never been anything but unrealities to us ill-educated men have to be reintroduced to our minds in some new and revealing way so that they will not be deprived of that shining beauty of reality which every detail of a first-born child has for its mother and which every detail of everything will presently have for the child, until mis-education dulls it.

This rebirth of lost perceptions is not to be had just for the asking. To scrap your old and feeble semi-comprehension of the natural things around you, and gain a happy new sense of the piquancy of their being just what they are—this is real regeneration, a rare and mighty operation of the spirit. All you can do to secure it is to keep your mind and body fit for a respectable spirit to enter, and then to go the right places. And none more right, for the purpose, than some road like this, along which all of central England that is not seen is implied, as the Apennines and the Alps are implied in the yellow and grey of the Tiber and Po. The gift may come while you grunt and sweat up the long rising road from Stockport almost to Buxton, right up one slant of England's roof. Or as your cycle slides obliquely down the eastern slant, beside the slowing streams and dropping voices of Wye and Derwent, through Derby and on to the high-pitched bridge, with a red inn upon it, at Shardlow, on the Trent. Or else at Kibworth Harcourt where, an hour's ride past Leicester, you surmount—almost imperceptibly, it is so low—the first of the four successive bars of higher ground that trend away crookedly before you, falling from the central heights on your right to the unseen but imaginable sea on your left.

Or at the roadside church in the Great Oxendon fields, where you cross the second of those bars, better warned of its nearness by a hard grind up the hill from Market Harborough, under great trees. Or where you cross the third, south of Northampton, a mile or two west of Cowper's Olney, and then run easily down to Newport Pagnell and the Ouse. Or, again, when the collarwork needed to lift you away from the Ouse has brought you up the banked stretch of road from Hockliffe to a nick in the chalk wall that forms the fourth. Or it may be at any point between these salient points; for the spirit of imagination bloweth as it listeth: it will not always choose what might have seemed to us its best opportunities.

V

In somebody else the mind may take light—the authentic light—from the look of the earth itself, its grain and colour, rather than from the modelling of its major contours. Till Stockport is passed, on your Londonward way, you notice the rich red sandstone in the railway cuttings and in the Mersey's trough. Beyond Hazel Grove the earth darkens, and used or unused collieries blacken each side of the road. Disley passed, they grow fewer and disappear; in their place you see the grit-stone quarries about Whaley Bridge and at Fernilee, as you toil up the five-mile hill. Through Monsal Dale and the Matlocks there is everywhere stone, but it becomes a different stone, whiter, more prone to stand up in broken faces beside the road, with ivy and bushes in its clefts, instead of slanting down to the road in bulgy slopes of wet moor. But from Matlock the rocks darken again and show less of those raw white surfaces; and soon, on the left as you pass Belper and Duffield, you spy the smoke of collieries before you set foot again, near Derby, on the red sandstone that you last saw near Stockport.

Red sandstone, coal, millstone grit, mountain limestone, millstone grit, coal, red sandstone—the order of their coming tells its own tale. You have crossed such an arch as one might make by pasting three layers of cardboard together, bending them into a semicircle, and then planing the top of this arch off till two of the three coats of cardboard were worn through and the third exposed. An insect passing over such an arch would traverse first the raw edge of the worn top layer, then the raw edge of the second, then an expanse of the now ex-posed lowest layer, then the raw edge of the second layer again, and finally the raw edge of the top layer again. The cyclist is the insect; the top layer is coal; the second layer is millstone grit; the third is mountain limestone. The three, laid flat on one another, have then been warped up into the Pennine arch, here called the Peak. Then the top of the arch has been scoured by the weather as if with emery-cloth, till first the coal and then the millstone grit (except one little piece, which forms Kinder Scout) have been worn clean through, and the third layer, the mountain limestone, brought to light. From Stockport to Whaley Bridge, roughly speaking, you cross the raw edge of the outermost layer, the coal measures; at Whaley Bridge and beyond you cross the raw edge of the second layer, the grit; at Matlock you are on the stripped surface of the third layer, the limestone, and beyond it you cross your two raw edges again, of course in inverse order, and finally, near Derby, you step off the arch on to the red sandstone that silted up round the base of the arch when its curve emerged above a sea that covered Stockport and Derby alike.

From Derby to London, a fresh spectacle awaits you. You traverse such a surface as is made when a six-volume book falls down sideways on a half-filled bookshelf, or when six paving-flags are placed against each other, standing on their edges, like a pack of cards, and then let fall. The first book or flag lies flat; the second leans upon the first and does not lie quite flat; the rest in turn lean on each other at the same angle, and the upper surface of the heap is rippled into a zigzag of rising and falling slopes, composed of the uppermost few inches of each slab, the rest of each slab going down out of sight between the slab it lies on and the slab that lies on it. Suppose now that the six flagstones were all of different degrees of hardness and that the general surface they present were roughly scoured and worn, so that the softer of the upturned edges would be planed away to dust while only the hardest slabs still presented their sharp ridges to the eye. That is what you see between Derby and London on this road. Beyond Leicester the red sandstone, on which you have been since Duffield, disappears, diving under the Lias rock or clay on which you gain a footing as you rise out of the valley of the Soar. Beyond Northampton the Lias in turn slips out of sight under the harder Oolites, which hold up a raw edge, cut across the grain, to face you at Edgehill and Naseby. Some five miles past Newport Pagnell the Oolites, too, take a plunge into the earth in front of you, and you quit them for the greensand under which they are lost, and which itself, a few miles farther on, at the rising stretch of road southward from Hockliffe, dips before your eyes under the great layer of chalk that takes its place as the outer coat of England. Now you are at Dunstable, and as you run down the softly undulating upper surface of the chalk, from there to St. Albans the soil dulls gradually from white to grey; the mud, if it be wet, grows less like cement; streams, which are scarce in chalk, now multiply again. Soon the chalk, like its predecessors, is done with, vanishing under the earth to reappear only beyond London, in the North Downs. From Ridge Hill, on the London side of St. Albans the straight, falling road carries your eye down into the great bowl of Lower Eocene clays in which London stands. Since you left Buxton you have set foot on nine of the known layers of the earth's crust, all in the order of their age, the oldest first, and each presenting itself as opportunely, when you have had time to digest the last, as a well-placed illustration to a lecture.

VI

Or, again, the spark may be struck in your mind by some momentary look that the road has, some trick of feature, or some significant mark. For the face of any old road is as visibly filled with expression and lined with experience as any old man's. Take the mere point of straightness and crookedness. A road, like a piece of string, goes straight when the strongest pull is from end to end; it goes crooked when the strongest pulls are to this side and to that. This great road north-westward from London is a string that once was pulled hard at the ends; then the end pull slackened and the lateral pulls increased; finally the end pull increased again; and so the one road is really found to be three: a Roman road that ran as the crow flies, its engineers thinking mainly of getting troops to distant stations; then a mediaeval and later road, used of course for through travelling also, but used still more for wayfarers from one country town to the next, and twisting from village to village, to right and left, for their convenience; finally, a modern coaching road of the fast mail-coach period, when once more the through traffic became relatively important, and the interests of villages a little off the direct route went down before the interests of travellers to Holyhead and Liverpool.

In plenty of places between Manchester and London you can easily see the straight Roman road and the crooked earlier English road running side by side, as they do not far from Rugby, or coinciding for a while, as they do in the great straight stretch—where there were few villages to give side pulls to the string—between Bletchley and Hockliffe. At other places—between Redbourne and Markyate, for instance—as you walk to London along Telford's great coach road you see on the left a grass-grown, twisty lane that was the main road once, now an almost unused path to a few cottages, and looking like those melancholy, amputated curves of the lower Irwell which now form only queer-shaped ponds, or "mortlakes," near the banks of the Manchester Ship Canal.

In at least one place in the latter part of the way from Manchester to London all three roads can be seen at once. When you have left London Colney and nearly reached the top of the long hill beyond, up which Telford carried a road of magnificent gradient and directness, a small byroad branches off on the right, apparently leading to a farm in a wood. Presently, if you look over the side of the embankment after topping the ridge, the half-disused ruts are again seen below, running ingloriously beside the great highway. A few yards more and this purposeless-looking track crosses the main road and goes off, deep in sand and arched over with hazels and oaks, to get at the gate of somebody's park. Three-quarters of a mile further on, at the foot of the hill, it is seen returning; again it crosses Telford's road, this time nearly at right angles, and visits the village of South Mimms, at a little distance to the right. That done, it is seen at once re-crossing the great road and traversing some charming country, where it serves a few houses, on the left. For the moment it then re-approaches Telford's road, but suddenly, as if remember-ing, just in time, that Wrotham Park (whose owner was perhaps chairman of Quarter Sessions) is half a mile away on the left, it goes off again at right angles, and is seen no more until it has made a roundabout entry into Chipping Barnet.

This picturesque by-lane, along which you must in many places wheel your bicycle, was the main road by which Swift travelled to Dublin. The great highway which cuts across its loops and windings as the upright lines in the dollar sign $ cut across the curved one is Telford's attempt to meet the demand for speedier travel between London and Holyhead. And all the while, a couple of miles to the west, the Roman road in the same direction is running straight as a ruler, but for the one sudden turn which looks as if it were intended not to lose the benefit of the particularly tough hill at Elstree. In the straightness of the straightest road of the three is written the nature of Roman rule in Great Britain, and in the modern straightening of the least straight is recorded the English settlement of Ireland, and perhaps the Act of Union.

There is no end to the expressiveness of ancient roads. They are all dinted with history; they echo with it. Even a literal dint may be found, in a field with brambles round it, not far from this road, where the earth has sunk in over the dead buried after Naseby. An echo resounds in the pure speech of the villagers of Northamptonshire, the most English of shires, where the Danish influence was weak and short, and whence came the form of English—the Tuscan of our Italian—that won back its place as the polite and lettered speech of the country two hundred and fifty years after the Conquest. It is audibly true now, as it was in old Fuller's day, that in Northamptonshire "the language of the common people is the best of any shire of England." A little further north along this road the very names of the places you pass through or near—Derby Ashby, Grooby, Amesby, Blaby, Frisby—are resonant of a complete Danish domination. In each of the three Midland counties that you cross—those of Derby, Northampton and Leicester—you find the county town placed almost at the middle point, like the navel in a bean. And the county is simply called after it. So that you scent pretty soon a county history shorter and simpler than that which has printed itself in the name and position of Chichester in a corner of Sussex, Exeter on the edge of Devonshire, or Reading in a bend of the Berkshire border.

With all the pretty and mind-stirring bric-a-brac of history the road is littered. Half-way up the steep slope that leads southward out of Northampton you spy on a bank among the trees, a few feet to the left, that best of all the crosses that Edward I. built wherever Queen Eleanor's bier was set down. A minute's walk to the east, as you cycle past Brixworth, you see a parish church partly built of Roman bricks as unmistakable as any on the Appian Way. For battlefields, you have the one at St. Albans whereon the Wars of the Roses opened, and near Northampton the one where Henry VI. was taken by the Earl of Warwick. Then you can trace, if you like, the Pretender's route from Manchester to Derby and weigh the credentials of that Leicester inn where Richard III. is said to have slept the night before Bosworth.

VII

You see—know the one thing, with the rich, living knowledge of sensuous contact, and you will know all. For all the rest is implicit in that one beloved part, as surely as life-changing things were implied in the single footprint that Robinson Crusoe found on the sand. To be able to see—really to see—the whole of some great thing with the mind, at the instance of some fragment seen with the eye—this is a kind of success in life; and not for the man of science alone, who in presence of one small remnant of bone fossilised in a cave can see the whole of a monstrous bulk that wallowed in warm prehistoric slime, but for the artist, the traveller, the common man with all the common things about him. To graft upon the bodily sense of sight a special kind of imaginative energy, so that when the fit eye has gone as far as it can, its work is taken over and carried on without a break; so that, when later you try to remember, you cannot say where physical perception stopped and where mental vision began—all you know is that between them they have left you the memory of expanses greater than bodily eye ever saw, and also more urgently real than imagination alone could ever frame; this is the key of the garden. Possessed to the full, it gives powers that cannot be stated without an appearance of rhetoric. "To see the world in a grain of sand, and heaven in a wild flower" is probably only a sober way of describing the visionary faculty of the collaborating eye and mind in a Blake. Many of us, I fancy, might attain it so far as to feel the whole modelling and structure of England in the labouring of the engine, and then in the effortless glide, as a train tops a great watershed; or to see all the enormous romance of the ascent from youthful to ancient states of the earth as the train goes north from London's bricky world of recent yellow clay, through the Midland shires where the red sandstone seems to have blossomed out above ground in the red roofs and walls of the towns, to the quiet grey of farms on Northern fells where every house is fashioned of bits of a rock that was made before the Alps.

CHAPTER X

ACROSS THE PENNINE

The deep, authentic mountain-thrill.
WILLIAM WATSON.

From gardens in Manchester suburbs your view to the east is closed by a long line of hill. It is less than twenty miles from you. No peaks stand out; the ridge runs almost level, due north and due south. This is the Pennine. It is an outlying bone of rock thrust down from the rocky mass of northern Britain into the soft flesh of England, somewhat as the Apennines are thrust down into Italy from the Alps. But the Apennines go all the way to the south; the Pennine goes only half-way; it ends north of Derby. It stands out from the English plain as the raised spine stands out from the back of a spade, declining in height till it disappears into the general level, near the spade's middle.

This English range is not built upon the grand scale, as mountain scales go. South of Whernside, Ingleborough and Pen-y-gent it does not rise above 2200 feet. The Peak, its last attempt to be high, before disappearing, runs to little more than 2000. That famous goose, Montgomery, Macaulay's butt, did his best to make a fool of the Pennine with indiscreet praise;

Here in wild pomp, magnificently bleak,
Stupendous Matlock towers amid the Peak;

Here rocks on rocks, on forests forests rise,
Spurn the low earth and mingle with the skies.

Great Nature, slumbering by fair Derwent's stream, Conceived these giant mountains in a dream. For any modest set of hills to be hymned to such tunes is no happiness; rather, a thing to live down. Still, the Pennine is mountain. It has a flora that runs to the Arctic Circle. When the sites of York Minster and Lancaster Castle were lying under the ice the Pennine rose above the general misfortune. Its veteran millstone grit stood out dark and unreddened by any geologic innovation throughout the time when a shallow sea was washing over all the lowland shires of the Midlands, narrowing to a strait at the gap where the London Midland and Scottish trains now pick their way between the Peak and the mountains of Wales, and laying down the red sands of which Chester Cathedral was in due time to be composed. You do find fossil shells of some sea creatures high up on the Peak. But these had lived in an older world untinged by such modernisms as begat the ruddy glow that now flushes the walls and roofs of Trent-side villages and the tilth of Nottinghamshire farms.

Above other invasions, as well as those of scouring glaciers and staining seas, the Pennine emerged inviolate. It let the Roman legions thunder by, beneath its flanks, and it waved Christianity aside. Against the Peak, its southern buttress, stream after stream of northward racial movement, peaceful or violent, broke and parted as currents do at the pier of a bridge. Celts and Romans and English, pushing out in turn from their south-eastern landing-places, would all seem to have paused, considered and then turned first to the left, the West, when they struck on the swelling tract of forest and rock that culminates in Kinder Scout. Romano-Celtic Christianity and Anglo-Saxon Paganism and then the Christianity of Augustine—all must have bumped up against the Peak and then coasted cannily northward, below its western slope, feeling their way towards the sea-board and Ireland.

A range of mountain may not be the Alps, and yet have a career. And the Pennine has done its big things. The way that its strata are bent and worn has shaped the industrial history of England. A kind of life that is not precisely lived anywhere else made the Brontes just what they were. On Pennine heights there stick out the raw ends of forces that help to set us all our work and to map out our lives. As you walk over Dead Head Moss, at the top of the ridge, on a wet day of southwesterly wind, you leave behind a steep, drenched western slant on which the wind has dropped most of its takings of water from the Atlantic. The cause of the different work and life of Yorkshire and Lancashire pours itself in at the doors of your senses; you see it in breaking clouds, hear it in the lowered voices of moorland streams and feel it in the slackening drip of rain-drops from a soaked cap to your nose.

Or go to Wharncliffe Crags upon the Yorkshire slope, east of Penistone. Here the infinite goodness and mercy of nature have made a rock-climber's gymnasium, three happy miles long, amidst fern and forest. If Paley had ever seen Wharncliffe, and been a rock-climber, his case might have been notably strengthened. The scrambler at Wharncliffe, resting midway up a smooth and square-cut "chimney," built for his use like a dream of desire, sees the moorland slopes below him sinewy and knotty with the twisted and notched roots that are still left of the chase where Gurth and Wamba talked together when Yorkshire was still roamed by droves of swine, like the Balkan forests to-day. From some two hundred yards below, across an intervening grit-stone quarry, there comes all day the whistling of engines busy in a siding; every few minutes some North Eastern train comes grunting up or sliding down the main highway of traffic between the two halves of the manufacturing North. From beyond the railway the climber hears in silent intervals the broken waters of the Don, whose pace was the fortune of Sheffield's first grindstones—perhaps cut from that quarry below. A few distant factory chimneys rise predominant over the smoke-filled hollows between sombre moors. In such a place you get an index or an epitome of North-West England. To Southerners it is a region of sharp surprises and piquant juxtapositions. Here English soil is more ancient than anywhere else, and the ways of man's labour more modern. For here alone the edges of towns where work is all a manipulation of steam and electric power are frayed against ridges of rock that were old before the site of London was made; here the factory hooter wakes sitting grouse and "you hear the clogs, before dawn, tapping a dotted line of sound through peat and bracken."

III

There was no bad wine in one's youth, and even to-day there is not such a thing as a bad mountain pass. The mere descent from one were joy enough to fill holidays—the easing of your breath, the flagging stride set suddenly free, the road that has begun to bear you of itself, as moving staircases do, down its unwinding coils, miles and miles of them on ahead, lying like tumbled white tape thrown on a floor, rising and falling, it seems to the eye, capriciously. Passes cannot be spoilt, not even if you waste half your attention on wheedling a car round the fifty sharp bends of the St. Gotthard zigzags, or free-wheel on a "push-bike" down the twenty-five lovely miles of the Grimsel's northern descent. But the sharpest delight of all attends the last stage of the rise. The surprise that your effort has earned is about to be paid you. The savour of contrast that all passes possess has matured: it awaits your absorption, not half a mile off. As you near the top, you feel that things are astir as if with some delicate sense of approaching event; cool air begins to lip over; it goes to your head; you exult to be reaching one of the spots where the make of the earth, its adventures and workings, come to a point and show themselves in their cunning variety and coherence. Perhaps, from the crest of the ridge that you are attaining, half of every pound of falling snow will be set apart to go to the German Ocean, and half to the Black Sea. Or you may look down, to right and left, on landscapes that speak of the Mediterranean of Titian and Vergil; and, again, of the Gothic North, its shrewd, astringent greys and its accesses of unsunned brooding and reserve. To this recondite height to which the tiniest streams resort, to collect the dues of the Danube and the Rhine, discordant civilisations come up almost visibly, too: across the edge of their desmesnes they look each other silently in the eyes.

Or things out of history may well come to life, in your mind, on some august pass. For, up here, history throngs. Over most of the surface of Europe it lies spread, as it were, pretty thin. Even in the Low Countries not every village is an Oudenarde, a Mons, or Waterloo. But European history poured deep and rapid, as rivers do with constriction, through a few straight defiles in the Alps. It comes lightsomely in to-day at the door of your mind when you top the highest point of some soaring track; why, Caesar too must have felt that the track was grievously long in reaching its summit when he was passing this way, to conquer the Gauls. And then you may fancy Franks flooding back over your pass, driving Lombards before them, and Charlemagne halting there, where you are, and seeing Italy, like you, for the first time.

IV

Of course no passes over the British Pennine have the certified fame of a Simplon, St. Bernard, or 'Stelvio. For no Papacy has resided below them on one side and no Frankish Kingdom on the other. So they did not have to be used, with all the publicity that could be got at the time, by world-shaking persons scuttling across in haste to be crowned, or to knock off the crown of a friend, or to take in a province. And yet—go to Wessenden Head or to the crown of Langsett Moor. You get the right feel of a pass:—the window is suddenly opened; the air comes blowing through; there is a thrill as of a curtain rising or of a chapter begun. You need no telling that here, where the cutting makes its sharper nick at the bottom of a gentle dip of the sky-line, there have, in all ages since man ceased to walk on all-fours, been considerable leapings of the heart and drawings of deep breaths. To this high nick, when things were quiet, little parties of Roman soldiers off duty will have made their way, following up the Etherow's banks from Mancunium to Longdendale head and then scrambling up among the trunks of the oaks that covered the last steep fell, till through a break in the trees they saw that the ground in front fell away, mile after mile, down to the level and unbroken floor of Yorkshire's sea of tree-tops. While waves of pitiless progress chased one another northward up the flatfish corridors below on each side, Piets and Brythons and Angles chasing and chased in their turns along the vales of Trent and York or through the Cheshire gap, you may fancy odd rags and remnants of out-manoeuvred races, forlorn defenders of lost causes, struggling up in flight to this parting-place of waters and peering over the summit ridge, wondering were any but enemies stirring in the unseen clearings below.

Perhaps we sup too full of records now, and fuss more than enough about a few grandiose historical "stunters" who snatched middle places on stages and made corners in limelight. A kind of insurgent equity rises at times in one's mind to plead for the more real makers of history, the privates who won the wars of the Napoleons and Caesars and all the millions of forgotten nobodies whose faithful rising to work before winter dawns enabled Papacies and Kingdoms to go on. And so, in an age of much vulgar screaming for vulgar attention, there even comes to be a subtle distinction attached to some beautiful road which only the obscure have trodden, so far as any one knows. Here at any rate the swelling hopes and quelling fears of the wayfarers, their quenched vivacities and their blistered soles have kept their dignity and passed on out of sight as little advertised as leaves that have lived out their lives at the centre of some unexplored forest.

The Pennine passes, too, are rich in that special regional savour of strange collocations. Coming west from Huddersfield by road, you mount long, gentle slopes, through verdure first and then over darkening moorland, the silence and solitude tranquilly deepening round you, up to the pass of Standedge. There the road tops the ridge by the help of a cutting. Suddenly, at the pass, everything changes. The chimneys and roofs of a great town are almost below your feet; snuggling under the western steep of the Pennine, Oldham puffs its contumacious smoke in the face of heaven; the cyclist feels he must jam on the brakes lest he fall into that reeking cauldron. Or you may ascend the easy and beautiful road over the moors from Ripponden to Blackstone Edge and tumble over the crest into Rochdale, after expecting anything but what you see.

V

So you are always brought back, within a few hours, to one or other of those two terms of a governing contrast—the bony hardness of England's North-western soil and the persistent hardness of man's work upon it. The coming of steam and its puissant successors has made, in one way, little difference. The flanks of the Pennine, in South-east Lancashire and the West Riding, are still the seats of exacting labour that they must have been before the first factory chimney astonished the hard-bitten moorland farmers round Glossop and Bolton. Frost and rain and earthworms have not had the time, even now, to weave a full coating of soil for the stone bodies of Tiviot Dale and Longdendale. Here, there and everywhere, some naked knee or elbow sticks out through the rock's skimpy clothing of moss and starved grass. Not easily can a man who farmed sheep on these hungry slants of hard stone, with some dirt clinging to them, have saved enough money to make an idler of his son.

And so it is to-day, with little difference. No doubt some idlers are made within sight of the Pennine. Since the Industrial Revolution plenty of cotton-spinners and other men, who perhaps were useful themselves in their day but grew rich and feeble, have failed to save their children, or perhaps even themselves, from the baseness of taking more from the world than they give it. But, happily, most of them fled from the place. You may find them scattered about England, spunging upon her; uneasy fugitives, they try to escape notice, and to forget what they were, in the disguise of feudal Wessex squires or heirs of Runnymede barons. So they help, in their own way, to heighten an exhilarating contrast that greets the migrant from London or some fashionable tract of the home counties to the sub-Pennine scene of mill and moorland, billberries and coal, where the fleeces of sheep are dirty with colliery smuts on the shoulders of a mountain, and a working spinner may look through the windows of his humid barrack at slopes ablaze with flowering heather and gorse. Up here, in normal times, every one seems to be either at work or else using with quiet and purposeful zest, or uproarious vehemence, some small interval for play.

In some pleasant parts of the south you may reasonably tremble for England. The life lived there, by nearly every one who has the power to live it if he chooses, is such that England only survives as a great figure in the world because far the greater number of her people either cannot or will not live in that way. In the battered ship that the war has left us to navigate, we are terribly crowded with otiose passengers. The playtime of hard workers is a delight to the observer's eye and ear and soul, but the unfortunates to whom the joy of some congenial hard work has never come are a rending spectacle for any one who has either a heart to pity the individual victims or an affection for the country whom they are failing. Most pitiful of all, perhaps, is the sight of the luckless young man or woman to whom no one has succeeded in showing any more stirring career of enjoyment than the continuous solicitation of what the sufferers pathetically call "having a good time," meaning the pursuit of happiness in disregard of the first condition of its attainment. At second-rate colleges in Oxford or Cambridge, in some parts of London for some months of the year, and in foreign places of common resort among the well-to-do

English of slight energy the ground seems almost to be littered with these failures, soldiers defeated before their first battle, incompetents listlessly and babblingly cumbering the decks of a ship cleared for action. What a set! What a use to make of the one chance we get of living with spirit! And what shall a country do in which it sometimes seems as if the invalid and unemployable minds and characters might actually outnumber and drag down the eager, skilful and strong?

In the working north the newcomer is rousingly relieved from the pressure of any such fears. The effect on your spirits resembles that of a front line in war, in contrast with that of a base. At the front every one is on trial, and any non-trier goes under or lives amid general scorn, a butt and byword. Little chance there for the clever dodger and loafer, the man who is only good to gossip or nag or blow bubbles of frail speculation while better men work. There a man must either give his proofs or be known for the worthless forked radish he is. Of course there are slackers and rogues to be found in a colliery district, and people may work as hard in a Tennysonian paradise on the South Downs as between the stone claws that the Pennine puts down on South Lancashire. Cheshire cheese hath its maggots as well as your Stiltons. And yet the northern air is different. You feel it blowing an astringent blast that makes you bestir yourself and want to be like those whom you see keeping their hands warm with work all around you. Like the Banished Duke, you feel you have got past the flatterers now. "New Counsellors" have come in to "feelingly persuade you what you are"; you have come face to face, more closely than ever before, with the exacting and bracing plight of man plumped down naked on a naked earth, soon to be dead unless he wins his own safety, and shamed if he tries to leave the winning of it to others.
You know the common kind of English novel—the scorn and laughing-stock of Canadian and Australian youth—in which the climax of the young hero's and heroine's romance is to come unexpectedly into a fortune which licenses them to be loafers together for life. There are some English places in which you can almost feel that this idea of success in life prevails beyond all others. To get a berth as parasite, to buy yourself out of the fight, to get quarters to sleep in and rations to draw, and never do a turn on guard nor shoulder a pack in return for it all—that would seem to be the aspiration nearest to the hearts of quite a host of puny shirkers. But carry it to the Pennine and rub it against the frayed edge of its stripped strata—the grit that makes millstones, the coal that drives factory engines, the mountain limestone that holds up the whole crushed Pennine arch for the coal to break through at the compound fractures on its flanks. Such a contact brings out, as by some chemical test, the ingredient of baseness in those squalid dreams of embezzled ease. It precipitates their ignobleness, as it were, in a turbid unmistakable cloud. They acquire the grotesque and ignominious look of a woman with a painted face, waddling on high heels upon a Cumbrian fell side. No one is wholly worthless while he stands on the tip of a great snow-mountain which he has climbed in spite of some tremors and much fatigue; even on our humbler Pennine your mind cannot grovel quite so readily as on some level patch of London clay.

VI

A year or two ago a man, whose record showed him to be no fool, and who had no sort of quarrel with life, set out alone in a storm, on a midwinter evening, to cross Kinder Scout. The Scout is the highest point of the Peak, and the last southern height of the Pennine. It used to be twice as high as it is. For years have planed a good two thousand feet of millstone grit and coal off the crown of the old Pennine arch. But at night, when snow is falling and shutting you up, as you walk, in a moving white cell, the black spongy peat flat that is now the top of the Scout has the right mountain glory of gloom. It raises the mountaineer's spirits as black frost without makes your fire burn better within. See Kinder Downfall with all the little precipice curtained with ice and hung about with pendant six-foot lustres of that crystal. Or in an equinoctial gale, when all the stream's water is caught by the wind at the edge of the fall and thrown back through the air onto the high table from which it has tried to lip over.

The man died of exposure that night, a few hundred yards from this spot. If he had reached it he would have known where he was and could have felt his way off the mountain. Many people said "Folly; a life thrown away," but others felt that a flame must have burnt pretty high in his spirit that night before it went out altogether. He asked for, and he must have got, his fill of the oldest and most elating of combative joys, the one beside which even Homer's "joy of battle" is a relatively modern substitute. To win that joy you need not even practise what counts, technically, as climbing—ascents of Matterhorns, Grepons and Drus and the like. Mere upland navigation will do. The Pennine gives plenty of room, when the right mood is on it. At some evening twilight, or morning of mist, you leave roads behind first, and then tracks, and strike into the open moor as a ship goes into the pathless Atlantic at night. Almost at once you are reposefully simplified; all that is complicated and inessential about you peels itself off, coat by coat, till, behold! nothing is left but a body as fit as your past may have made it, an eye to read map and compass and watch, a brain to connect what you read, and a will to go on in absolute faith in those three. No gallery either, no impertinence of fussy help or intrusive counsel. You are for the moment alone in Columbus' cabin; play, the most serious thing in the world, has made you one, in your own little way, with all who have found their good in going into the dark by themselves to wrestle with those queer-tempered angels the earth and the sky. Your legs and your wits and your compass may lead you through darkness and tempest over the top of Kinder to a thawing-place in Edale's friendly inn, or through falling snow across the Adler Pass to Saas Fee, or across an uncharted sea to a new world, but still the essential thrill is the same, the delighted spirit's exultation in the prevalence of your simplest powers over the brute resistance of nature.

Bergson suggests that we like tragic plays because they awake in our retentive, long-pedigreed souls an elating sense of the harsh and sombre youth of our race—of the terrible fellows we were when a man would fight a friend to the death for the hide of a slaughtered wild horse, or woo him a bride by stunning her with a club and bearing her home over his shoulder through all the miles of forest between the young people's several kraals. The joy of the duel with hard weather may be "residual" too. The solitary mountain rambler of to-day may be unconsciously trying to dig up and enjoy the long-buried rapture of that first father of his who ventured westward up the steep forested slope of blackering earth above the red Cheshire sands and peered over the Pennine ridge, between the trunks of the Peak Forest oaks, at the gentler slant running down east into the Yorkshire to be. Anyhow, he has made an escape. He has got out of reach, for the day, of that besetting malady of intricate civilisations—the want of a stirring visible relation between effort and result. A typical modern figure is the municipal Medical Officer who half thinks that his preservative work for the frail may only be compromising the future of the race. Matthew Arnold described it all, wailfully well, in his plaint about the way that we "each half-live a hundred different lives," strive without quite knowing what we strive for, and doubt and fluctuate and make fresh starts and then have fresh misgivings and nag and chatter and rant about ideals we do not live up to, until we "falter life away" with little done. At least for some eager and absorbed hours your true rambler has washed all that futilitarianism out of his soul and has started fair again in a heaven of simple effort and clear aim; a career in life opens before him at breakfast; success in life warms him at bedtime. He has discovered a way of playing from which most ways of working have something to learn—concentration and joy and the sense of an absolute value in any hand's turn that is done with a will.

"I had never," a modern philosopher wrote from the Alps some years ago, "been before on the sort of places we went up—mostly rocks—and I found it as much as I could do. But I got better as I went on, and am certainly glad of the experience. I don't think I can ever get along without occasionally doing something physically violent. It seems necessary to prevent thought from degenerating into flabbiness. Or rather, perhaps, it helps me to realise that the qualities wanted in what are called 'physical efforts' are really just as much wanted in what are called 'mental.'" Two years later he died of exposure in a storm on Mont Blanc, just as the man did on Kinder. That such things should sometimes—very seldom—befall, in this greatest of sports, as well as in hunting and football and swimming and every great sport you can name, is nothing against it or them. The mere retention of life is never a big enough aim to absorb all its powers. And even here it may count for a little that death by a fall on a mountain, or by exposure on one, is as a rule, death disarmed, for the dying, of many distresses—those that you know when you see men die, as the grimly ironical phrase is, "quietly in their beds."

If we all knew the dates of our deaths and could choose only the manner, who would take long over the choice? On the one side the stilled, unnatural room; the long, slow losing fight for breath; the lonely waiting, perhaps, in a kind of ante-chamber to extinction, impenetrable by your friends; perhaps worse. On the other an Enoch's translation from the full height and heat of radiant vigour, effort and joy: an instant fall down two thousand feet of ice or rock wall into peace, or the restful collapse of all the muscles into the acquiescence of bodily exhaustion; and this in no smothering prison of curtains and lamplight, but with the sane and clean touch of sun and wind on you still, perhaps with the blown granules of ice lightly stinging your cheek as you take your departure.

And here indeed might Death be fair If death be dying into air,
If souls evanished mix with the Illumined heaven, eternal sea.

The handsome lines recur to the mind as you think of an ending so clear of the minor charges, at least, that most of us have to bring against death.

Still, death may be met at any turn of a street and has nothing especial to do with the rambler on mountains, those vivifiers of life. For life is nowhere more itself, its hardy, invincible self, than on the crown of the Pennine. There the land lies black for mile after mile of soaked bog, just endless hummocks of peat, the whole waste reticulated and sluggishly drained by ditch-like depressions which moat each hummock off from the rest and receive the sullen brown oozings from its saturated tissues. The place, if you give it only a summary glance, may seem morose, lethargic, almost dead. Looked at more closely it becomes the scene of endless gallant or stoic contrivance, the dodges and shifts of unbeaten stickers to life. Bilberries, heather and sedges have made themselves leathery coats, like the airman, to keep out the cold when the ground shall lie for months under snow; bog moss and cotton grass have renounced the delicate and dressy tints of their kindred who live in luxurious lowlands; all crouch low, bracing themselves compactly to hold together in the furious winds that scrape mountain ridges; they keep their leaves narrow and wiry, taking no needless risks of expansion; most of them drive deep roots far into the stony ridge's thirty-foot coating of peat, mindful of the searching droughts when that mighty sponge, wet through and through for most of the year, dries down to depths at which earth is never dry in the plains. Up here a splendid hardihood is always showing, as men sometimes show in a shipwreck, a famine, or a war, the enormity of the vicissitudes which the stubborn will to live can adapt the feeble body to endure. And under foot, wherever you go, is that singular monument of the continuity and the un-quenchableness of life, the peat itself, in which the roots of mosses that grew ten thousand years ago are still so intimate a means of life to mosses green above them to-day that you can hardly feel any part of the whole mass to be quite dead. Layer after layer, the leaves of to-day become the wet-nurses of the leaves of to-morrow. Tomorrow over, they bear up the nurses of yet another generation and keep their breasts from running dry. Nothing comes to be without a function in that tribal life of the bog, although its function may change. It is as if the joint life of a race, or of mankind, could become visible at the same time, in its whole evolution, so that we should see quite easily how much we incline to overrate the completeness and importance of death. It may be no great things that are brought to an end when it comes; and much may yet be done by those whom it has visited.

CHAPTER XI

Such a man, sir, should be encouraged; for his performances show the extent of the human powers in one instance, and thus tend to raise our opinion of the faculties of man. He shows what may be attained by persevering application; so that every man may hope that by giving as much application, although he may never ride three horses at a time, or dance upon a wire, yet he may be equally expert in whatever profession he has chosen to pursue.
DR. JOHNSON, on Circuses.

I

For most of us commonplace men—I am not so sure about women—the way of life that is most profoundly and durably pleasant, for most of our time, is that of the ordinary English country house. It satisfies the greatest possible number of the wants of the average man and gives generally healthy play to the greatest possible number of his sane impulses. That worthy is not a deep student or thinker; nor is he an absolute saint; his body has much more to do with him than theirs has with them, though he is no mere creature of sensual appetites either. He feels the various engines of his body and his spirit to be running their best in this life of rude health, of effort mainly physical, and not exhausting at that, of easy and unexacting social activity, of unmistakable personal consequence, and all these amenities flavoured with a certain consciousness of well-doing by the addition of some light and un-perplexing public duties. To be healthy and well amused and always respectfully treated, and also to feel that you are the backbone of your country—what decent ordinary man would ask for more?

To satisfy these standard needs of the body and the soul the patient constructive instinct of our well-to-do has built up, story by story, through the centuries, the most agreeable of all human mansions. Admire the quiet stability—alas! now shaken at last—of the old squirearchical life, broad-based on land and beeves. Wealth set like a gem in a matrix of surrounding poverty; power raised into effective relief against spacious backgrounds of helplessness and dependence; wherever you move, the never-staling myrrh and frankincense of the touched cap and the bobbing curtsey; and yet no feudal insolence of domination to turn your own stomach against these offerings of the lowly; everywhere the subtle semi-conscious prudence of the English squire, in league with the inherent decency of human kind, has slowly worked out the relation of rural landlord and tenant into a form almost easy, often almost affectionate. The English genius of moderation, never far from the ear of the right English squire, tells him precisely how far he can go without forfeiting the inestimable sensation of being a good fellow at bottom and seeing this cherished image of himself reflected in the faces of his dependents and bedesmen.

All your time is your own. No inexorable morning train or factory hooter reminds you daily of the curse laid on Adam. And yet you are rescued from any dis-comforting sense of being an idler, a mere passenger on the ship. At lenient intervals there are sittings of summary courts and of Councils, major and minor, which you can attend if nothing serious prevents, and renew your sense of the terrible fix in which people would be, but for you. All going well, your income—a sordid detail, but what would you? a fellow must live—comes in of itself; your plough, as they used to say, goeth of Sundays; and yet you are spared any painful suspicion that you are a maggot, perhaps, in your dear country's cheese—an apprehension too apt, in this heyday of conscience, to visit those unfortunates whose income arrives by post, out of the void, in the form of dividend warrants from institutions with which they carry on no human relations. Somehow it seems as if you must be doing a world of good to the worthy farmers whom you allow to remain as your tributaries; you feel as radium in a hospital may feel while it distributes physiological benefits around it, itself remaining in repose. And then there are the hunting, the shooting, the long days in the air, every one different from all the rest, and every one the same, as far as differentness and sameness can be the more delicious; and then the flush of health which comes of such days, the glow akin to that which follows a good hard game of football and a bath, with its extraordinary similarity to a just consciousness of moral beauty.

I think of moments in November woodlands—the early-failing day; the mists; the last few linked or single detonations of guns; the first lights coming out in the Jacobean house silhouetted against the western crimson; the shooting party silent perhaps, but plunged in the restful contentment of men who all day have been giving its fill to a deep residual instinct no longer beset with the worries that used to attend its operation when he who could not kill his beast had to go empty-bellied; all play now, and yet all a-tingle, as the best play is, with jocund intimations of the thrill of authentic hazards and desperate adventure; out here, in the winter evening's astringent air, the painless vision of man's hard early life, with every meal to be hunted and each winter's frosts to be cunningly and laboriously kept from congealing his blood in its courses. And over there, where the lamps within are beginning to show the mullions barring crosswise the luminous swell of the great oriel windows, under the snug dormered roof of the hall and the playful spiral flutings of its busy chimneys, the sum and expression of all that in millions of years man has done not only to satisfy those primal needs but to crown their satisfaction with every grace and fantasy of pleasantness devisable by art.

For all the arts have laboured together to bring to perfection this masterpiece of intelligent energy in the pursuit of sane pleasure. The mother art of architecture turned away from the making of marvellous houses for God to plan mansions equally perfect for the Tudor lords of English manors. Like Medici in Florence and Bourbons in France, the great English squire set to work the men who, if born in the heyday of faith, would have been building cathedrals like Durham and York. Vanbrugh, the Adams and Gibbons were lions under his throne. For painters from Vandyke to Sargent the amplitude of his rural quarters made galleries such as town houses can seldom afford. Recent auctions have amazed connoisseurs of such things with a new sense of the multifarious wealth of the English art of furniture design. Of course some great country houses are stocked with sad rubbish. Of course, again, some modern heirs of rural museums of purest treasure are divertingly insensible to the beauty of their belongings. But still this little world of choice things has grown on and on, as the Venice that we now see grew up in the hands of rich men who cannot all have been critical exquisites.

Poets came in to enhance with the expression of their own enjoyment the beauty and the comfort that they found in Haddon and Montacute, Temple Newsham and Bolsover, Hatfield and Stowe. And, all the time, the special English art of narrative fiction has had its eyes fastened fondly, almost adoringly and certainly adorningly, on this peculiarly English social product. Fielding chuckled over it in its rude youth; Jane Austen steeped it in the vibrant sunshine of an affectionate irony; Thackeray and George Eliot, while casting dissimilar eyes on its germs of decay, delighted, in spite of themselves, in the mellow old-masterliness of its scenes and properties. As the dissipations of eighteenth-century London live in the prints of Hogarth and the blackguard yarns of Smollett, so the Augustan noon-tide and early afternoon lustre of the English country house will survive in the Victorian novels; Mr. Galsworthy has crowned the long series with those of his books and plays which show the country house overshadowed and fey, like one that fears he has outlived his time and sees the ordered pleasaunces of his life invaded by chilling portents of dismantlement and disarray.

II

Little need we wonder if in the country house there has sometimes prevailed a somewhat Olympian tone when these practitioners of happy, healthy and well-conducted play are speaking about compatriots so far misguided as to live and work and rear their broods in Midland and Northern "black countries." Who so base as live in Sheffield? It does seem almost unworthy. What can lead hundreds of thousands of persons to pass the whole of their lives within the sound of tramcar gongs or to go in by crowded suburban trains on six days out of seven to work with their heads well down over desks, under extravagant pressures of carbonic acid? Some, no doubt, are forced by poverty; yet there are others, unsought volunteers of stuffiness, who follow these ignoble courses without the pressure of actual want. With all the delectable mountains of the world to feed on, what but some defect of nature or some taint of blood can make men wilfully elect, like the elder Hamlet's misguided widow, to "batten on this moor"? To people that have always lived in excellent air, with a noble expanse of pinewoods in view from the drawing-room window, these incorrigible denizens of ugliness are apt to present themselves as standard social guys, mis-understanders of life and meet objects for genial satire. You find a kindred feeling of disdain in the well-bred person, described by Shakespeare's Hotspur, who came up during an interval in the battle, from some agreeable place in the rear, and was rather critical and superior about the nasty, unhandsome ways and belongings of the front-line troops. Perhaps our front-line troops, the hard-bitten dwellers in smoke-canopied towns, who carry on England's somewhat exacting war against national poverty and decay, are not crushed to the earth when they hear a refined voice remarking that theirs is a shabby pursuit for any one to addict himself to. But the censure, though lost on its objects, may give the critical person some happiness. And all happiness counts, and, especially, no harmless little gratification should be denied to the dying.

For dying, alas, the country house is. Its present rapid decline had to come. The war only hastened a process of decomposition already begun. A chilly fear had already crept in that the old squirearchical life, so buxom, blithe and debonair, was really a glorious piece of indulgence which England could only afford in the old days of her easy primacy in wealth; it would have to pass from us if ever the nation felt, through all its ranks, the real pinch of impoverishment. Few of us, too, could feel any longer the easy, happy certitude that most of our forefathers felt about the decency of perpetual and unqualified family ownership of great possessions. In nearly all of us there has been shaken, if not shattered, that happy, uncritical assumption that the common rural magnate with his cheerful, bracing consciousness of a beneficent stewardship, his picturesque passion and talent for sport, and his light, congenial labours of local administration, was really radiating round him all the economic and moral benefits that he supposed. Many of us hung on hard to the hope that a life so intensely and durably delightful could also be one of indispensable public service. There was an undeniable charm about the idea that you could make yourself a real vertebra in the backbone of your country by hunting on four days a week, shooting on one, and riding in on another to imprint your darling conception of corrective justice upon proceedings at petty sessions. If only all the practice of virtue were so agreeable!

Then came the war, like a precocious frost that kills in September geraniums that anyhow would have had to die in November. The typical "residential, sporting and agricultural estate," as a solvent concern paying its own business outgoings and the expenditure of its owner on a traditionally expensive and handsome manner of life, had visibly used up its fitness to survive in the environment that fate had brought to it. As a private hobby kept up with the proceeds of urban ground rents, or of royalties on coal, or of some lucrative operation carried on in a town, the thing might live on, for a while, as giraffes and gazelles can be kept alive, at some cost, in the Zoos of countries where they can no longer live wild. But the funeral bell began tolling as soon as the Allied victory on the Marne in 1914 had run its limited course and the Germans had settled themselves into their trenches between the Alps and the sea. Thenceforth the war must be one of attrition, life against life, purse against purse. It might leave us with only a quarter of our old incomes taken away, or a third, or a half. But any of these heroic diminutions would suffice to throw out of gear the precariously geared finances of English country houses whose owners could not subsidise them from somewhere outside the ring of farms that were their provinces. The nipping frost had come and the geranium's summer was over.

Perhaps our regrets for this casualty of the war ought not to go further than does our pensive regard for the picturesque windmill that age has clawed in his clutch. We do not seriously insist that all our corn should still be ground by Zephyr, Boreas and those other tall fellows their kindred. We could not pay the price of the bread. And even before the war began shaking our old and romantic land system to pieces, it gave us a mournful kind of anaesthetic to lessen the shock of the big operation. It furnished sadly good reason to think that our old rural world was not quite what we had fondly supposed.

Many had clung, at any rate, to a vision of our Arcady as a nursing mother of the sturdiest and fittest manhood in the world. The war ended that. It exposed our nurslings to merciless competition with those of Canada, Australia and New Zealand. In Belgium and France you saw the home-born and the oversea-born marching past each other on the roads, or fighting on each other's flank, or just using their leisure to look about a strange land. And then the truth could not be blinked. We had failed to give our rural "common people" what every man ought to have and what few of their oversea comrades had not. Ours had not the stature and strength of the others, their rude vitality, their alertness, their nervous resilience, their eager mental curiosity and their rich reserves of initiative, ingenuity and sense. However little an English witness might like it, he had to feel that the life of the English village, in which he had probably taken at least some sort of aesthetic delight, was not fit to compare with the life of small Canadian farms or wide Australasian sheep-runs as a mould for turning out men fit to get the most out of life and to make the best job of it.

War is not everything, nor need the best soldier be at all other times the best man. But the points where we made a poor show in the war were mainly points of sheer arrest in development; our youths were relatively stunted; something seemed to have got in their way before they could become, in the proper course of mental and moral growth, as self-reliant and as quick to take new means to new ends as the youths from Canada and Australia who made it so painfully plain that they thought of "Tommy" as undersized in body and mind. Now that fate, and no wisdom of ours, is forcing us to re-make our rural England, on pain of seeing its ruins lie about on the ground, let it cheer us as much as may be to reflect that what we have lost is not a thing of mature perfection, but only a thing which had, relatively to others, failed in its principal function of turning out men fit to stand with the best.

III

Yet regret cannot wholly be banished. It is not often for merit that people are loved. It is mostly because, as Falstaff says of one of the lovable, these have "given us medicines to make us love them," good or bad. No doubt the fairest of the ancient coaching inns, to outward view, were sometimes kept by harpies; the village stocks may well have been, when in use, a pretty brutal affair; the squire of some estates a petty tyrant or dull boozer; the whole bucolic concern, when brought into the thin dry clarity of utilitarian lamplight, an affront to reason and conscience. And yet who shall disclaim a sneaking sympathy with the delicious thrill of insight into an older world that shakes the American tourist at sight of these English curiosities? They tickle that amateur of ancientry who forms a considerable part of each of us. Something which is rather knowledge of the world than sentimentality assures us that the inherent good nature of man, which always tends to soften human relations of long standing, must have kindled many warm regards between members of the different classes that met each other in the common interests of husbandry and sport.

And then there is the irresistible effect of our knowledge that the greater English country house is really dying. We nearly always contrive to think of the dying with some charity. However imperfect their past performance, their one chance is gone now; their great adventure is over, and if they have mulled it you feel it hard that none of us can have a second try. Probably no British architect will ever again have a commission to build a rural palace for a private owner. Other grand or grandiose things he may have to design, but not a Chatsworth or a Castle Howard. These and their like will pass into the condition of Leonardos and Rembrandts, of which one may at any time expire by fire or senile decay, but no more can in any way be born. For the attitude of Hamlet towards marriage in a dislocated Denmark is that of our impoverished and irritated age and nation towards these monumental expressions of individual wealth and complacency; those that are built shall remain, but let there be no more of such buildings. The whole chapter is written; we read it with some touch of the tenderness due to a mighty plan that must now abide by whatever befell it in the course of its execution. We trace with gusto the growth of the country house from the early mediaeval family fortress to the late mediaeval manor-house like Haddon; and then on, through the stately and yet home-like and lovable Elizabethanism of Montacute, Longleat and Knole and the heavier grandeurs compiled by Vanbrugh and Inigo Jones, to such modern confessions of artistic embarrassment as Waterhouse's Eaton Hall.

Of course the coming architects will have great things to do. If no one will ever build for himself in London another Somerset House, still the London County Council's new riverain home is a pretty large load for any one man to be commissioned to lay upon the earth. The new cathedral at Liverpool is to be larger than either St. Paul's or York Minster: St. Peter's alone will be larger. Our railways have scarcely begun to build ambitious terminal stations as the Americans do. If "big business" ever picks up enough strength, in a lean post-war world, to resume its practice of growing bigger and bigger by eating little businesses up, we may yet have an English firm giving to an architect a job as wonderful as Nash's commission to design all Regent Street. The possibilities opened to art by the modern rebirth of "town-planning" are glorious. Only the major country mansion seems likely to atrophy. Soon such deposits as Audley End, Burghley and Blenheim may come to be cherished as documents recording a social state as incapable of revival as those which left for their expressive monuments the Pyramids and the Parthenon.

The old feudal England, beautiful and somewhat naughty in her day as some old women have been in their prime, died of malnutrition during the war. A handsome old witch, hard and game to the last, she had long been bedridden and lean as a rake, but always rouged herself to see the doctor and flouted fate with a will. We may think of her now with Mary Stuart and Cleopatra and Helen, ladies whose looks were so good and their frailties so sturdy that time itself has been corrupted into giving them a kind of shrift and admitting them to a calendar, not exactly of saints, but of supremely piquant awakeners of imagination. I stood the other day in the great court of a monastic-looking private house to which Charles II. once bolted to get away from the Plague which his subjects and neighbours in London were then more or less manfully facing. The great yews near me had their roots wrapped round the bones of the yet older chantry with which a Plantagenet King had sought to bribe God to connive at his having acquired his throne through a murder. Overhead, on a roof, there swaggered a monstrous stone heraldic beast that had looked down from another roof at the bonfires blazing beside Charing Cross for the Stuart Restoration and then for the acquittal of the seven bishops and then for the coming of William and Mary. The vast house was empty, its blinds down, its doors rigidly closed. So it remained through all the years of a generation except on two midsummer days in each year. On these its owner gave two garden parties, the blinds were opened and guests flitting through rooms and corridors glanced hastily at the masterpieces of the brothers Adam interned in this damp fastness. In all that unused place there was no sound now except the whispering plash of a thin fountain playing in the middle of the court and the tread of a sparrow on dry fallen leaves. Outside, the park, forbidden to all, seemed almost to moulder on this autumn afternoon with derelict stillness, a kind of inanition, the lapsing of some functionless organ into decay. Beyond its walls children, I knew, wriggled and snarled in the cramped slums of a slatternly town that had always seemed to live languidly and grimly under the shadow of this huge house, like the grass under a tree that keeps rain and dew out. All horrible, in a way, all crying out to be changed and made un-wasteful and fair. And yet something works through men's meanness and greed as well as their generosity,

Brings freedom with the tyrant's chains
And wisdom with the fool.
The jealous vanity of a rich family, void of comradeship

with countrymen and neighbours, had built up, cell by cell, the sinister, sequestered beauty of this solitude islanded in the midst of crowds. Some unseen "producer," as it were, had transmuted into a thing of delicate melancholy and pensive charm this sum of many centuries' expression of a tawdry pride and a timorous instinct of exclusion. The heaviest tombs beside the Appian Way can in some sense appeal to us, even while we feel that they were somewhat sorry souls who put up those hulking bids for immortality. Like Louis's Versailles and Wolsey's Hampton Court, the country houses of the English "ruling class," now almost dispossessed, may be finer than their makers. As rulers these have possibly failed; but as foxes or rabbits engaged in the immemorial task of making themselves as snug as they could, they mastered their job and did wonders. They must have given themselves some marvellous days in the air and nights at the table and even in the library. To-day, as your eye wanders over their ranges of stables and cellars, the cunning, long-disused ice-houses half interred in their parks, the generous scale of their kennels, the amplitude of their open fire-places, their kitchens and gun-rooms, you can regret nothing. For you would be worse off to-day if you were without the idea you get from these things of the measure of man's iron will and versatile power to give himself a good time. That any one should ever have done that particular thing so shrewdly well enlarges your vision of human accomplishment.

CHAPTER XII

THE FACES AND FORTUNES OF CITIES

There, where the long street roars, hath been
The stillness of the central sea.
TENNYSON.

I

Any one can perceive the historical fragrance of places like Winchelsea and Montreuil, Ravenna and Rye. Once on a time they were ports with the sea deep at their quays; the sea made them great. Now they are far inland: in none of them will you hear on the roughest day the sound of a wave. The sea gave and the sea has taken away. Yet they survive, pensioned off as it were, and living, in a modest way, a pensive and dignified life, like the old soldiers at Chelsea. Long sequestered from the hustle and racket of the central stream of urban progress, they sit apart in their archaic clothes, quietly brood in the sun and tell stories of their great youth to the eager amateurs of the antique who come to converse with them.

Yet their cases are not singular; only a little extreme. The special causes that once made a site peculiarly good for a town are always passing away and giving place to causes which make some other site better. It is not the sea alone that recedes. London herself, as well as Rye, has long survived the state of things which caused her to be exactly where she is. On London Bridge, as well as on the ramparts of Montreuil, which once had the sea at their feet, you may feast your fill upon thoughts about the perishableness of the raisons d'etre of cities. Your mind may cast back to the earliest bodies of Continental entrants into our island. Not liking to lose sight of land, they would cross to England south of the Thames, probably by that route, from Calais to Dover, to which human frailty still assures primacy. But their hearts would be set on the good things that they had heard to be awaiting them north of the Thames, the fat, flat, sunny cornlands of East Anglia, still the teeming mother of the best English wheat. So the thing they wanted to do, from the moment they came ashore, was to find a ford where an army could wade across the Thames, or a gut where they might bridge it.

II

With his fancy warming to the work, the musing person sees the newcomers feel their way westward along the south bank of the Thames. They are constantly thwarted. They cannot even get near the deep waters in mid-stream. Miles of squelchy riverain marshland hold them off. Now and then hope rises, where a spit of hard gravel or chalk sticks out like a pier into the river through the boggy alluvial clays of its south bank. The leader marks down one of these piers at what is now Gravesend, another at Greenhithe, another at Erith, and two more at Woolwich and Greenwich. He wades out from the tip of each spit, but soon finds he is swimming. He ferries himself across in a native coracle to see if there be any hope of throwing a bridge, for his host and its baggage to cross. No, plague take it! Opposite each of the piers jutting out from the south there is on the north bank nothing but that endless clayey morass: a bridge would have to be miles long. He reconnoitres the northern bank as well as he can and finds a couple of those bony natural piers there too—one at Grays, as we call it, another at what we name Purfleet. But none of these piers jutting southward is opposite any of the piers jutting northward. All no good. "Will Fortune never come with hath hands full?" So, like the sick king, the early invaders of Britain may reasonably have asked as they groped and sounded their way along the river boundary of Kent.

And then at last Fortune did come full-handed. Out through the spongy alluvial clays on the southern side a ridge of hard sandy gravel projected northward, carrying the explorers dry-shod to, at least, the edge of the open river. And right down to the water's edge, exactly opposite, upon the northern shore, there sloped, steep and dry, another bank or ridge of hard gravel. At last nature had vouchsafed the two abutments needed for a bridge. Along the crown of that southern ridge of gravel and over London Bridge to gain the northern ridge of gravel, a morning host of City clerks troops to-day. Though neither King William Street, E.C., nor the Borough High Street presents a gravelly appearance to these wayfarers' eyes, the site of the world's greatest city was thus determined some millions of years before, by a seeming caprice in the earth's distribution of gravel, sand, alluvium and Eocene clays. When once the luck came, it came in abundance.

A natural waist in the Thames, a geological invitation to the bridge-builder, was to be found at Battersea too, and an easy ford at Brentford. Still, the first bridgeable place was the thing. The lowest easy crossing over a great river is like the eldest son of a peer: everything goes to each of these two, though the one be only the first by a mile and the other the eldest by five minutes. Like Bristol and Norwich and Lincoln, Canterbury and York, Rochester, Chester and Exeter, London got her chance in life by being the first bridge town upon a river navigable by sea-going craft. Every one of that august company has its cathedral and bishop and great historical glories, although the original reason for its importance has long passed away or declined. Nearly all of them wear something now of that Chelsea pensioner look. More or less, the world has passed them by—a world they partly envy and partly disdain, feeling it ugly and raw as compared with their fair, mellow selves, and yet ruefully feeling, besides, that it seems in these vulgar times to have more of a function than they—to be, as the people of science say, more wholly organic.

III

Iron ore is not rare: rust-red brooks may be seen almost anywhere. So, when we in this island first took to iron, we did not mine it at places like Cleveland or Furness, where the deposits of ore are specially rich. We just got it out of the ground as near as we could to places where there was plenty of fuel to use for smelting it. All fuel was wood at the time; so the smelting of iron throve most where there were goodly forests to turn into firewood—in the West-country Forest of Dean, in Shakespeare's Midland Forest of Arden, and in the forests then covering the Kent and Sussex Weald. That early stage of industry, like others that have passed away, left its own deposit of towns bearing names that now sound somewhat patrician; they are well weathered by history; yet they show little now to account for their hoary prestige.

Then came coal, to redistribute fortunes among places as well as men. No doubt, wherever primeval forest has been, there may well be coal too. For seams of coal are the natural family vault of a forest of very long lineage. Plenty of coal, in fact, underlay all those three famous forests. But it was at different depths. Under the Weald it was too deep to mine with the mining plant we had then: we are only just broaching our Kentish coal now. Under the Forest of Dean it was workably near the surface, and so the local iron industry hung on and used the new fuel. The Forest of Dean is a big coalfield still, though not one of the greatest. Under the Forest of Arden, or its surroundings, the coal was found gloriously easy to get. The iron ore, too, in those parts came to hand readily. So Birmingham, neighbour to Stratford-on-Avon, rose into greatness when she had no longer to burn for her smelting any of the many trees on which Orlando carved Rosalind's name. Relatively to Birmingham's booming prosperity the Forest of Dean iron trade languished and that of Kent and Sussex died. The Weald and Gloucestershire towns inclined towards the condition of dowagers, portly and pleasant, but now without a future, and a little overblown. Round the great new coalfields upstart towns leapt out of the earth.

Then came steam, and presently all wholesale industry seemed to be making a rush for the coal. Where the fuel was, the heart was also. Cotton fastened on the coalfield of the Pennine's western slope, happy to have it in the damp region that spinners of cotton prefer. Wool took the coal that cropped out on the eastern slant of the same range. Iron kept the Midland coalfield between Cannock Chase and the Clent Hills. Cotton, wool and iron, all together, descended upon the coal basin of Lanarkshire. To »this epoch, when industry rushed to wherever coal was, we owe the middle-aged part—and it is much the larger part—of the Birmingham, Manchester, Glasgow and Leeds that we know.

At length that coal-chasing impulse fell off. Many new forces assisted to check it. Cases arose where it seemed signally gainful to cart the coal to the raw material instead of carting the raw material to the coal. Better to smelt the teeming iron ores of Cleveland and Furness at Middlesbrough and Barrow with coal brought by train from Durham and Whitehaven than to transport the ores, with all their waste dead-weight, to some distant coalfield. Besides, in the thronged old seats of manufacture, rents and rates were going up; many costs of production were pretty constantly rising. Leaders of industry asked themselves whether it might not be cheapest to get away from the crowded towns into the country, even though it meant going a little way off from both raw material and coal. So long as they had a main line of railway passing their doors, and perhaps a canal, the net result might be gain. The railways led the way by placing their private seats of industry at such places as Swindon and Crewe, to which almost everything had to be carried by rail. And now new factories and works are springing up in the fields along all the great railway lines, many of them just a little outside towns like Reading and Rugby, Northampton and Bedford, not of the first industrial order. Industry shakes itself out more loosely; it ceases to huddle round certain sources of things that it needs.

IV

What will come next? Are we likely to go on much longer carrying coal all over the country at heavy cost, when we know already that its latent power and heat can be extracted from it at the pit-head— presently, perhaps, even at the bottom of the shaft or—who knows?—in the seam where it lies unhewn? When the force to drive an engine is distilled out of coal at the pit and circulated by wire to every part of the country, one of the bigger causes that now control the fortunes of cities and towns, making them wax and wane, exalting them into improvised Babylons and dismissing them to a dignified or squalid retirement, may be almost abolished. It seems possible that manufacturing industry, as distinct from commerce, may lose altogether its habitual association with towns, as it is almost certain to lose its trailing clouds of smoke. Seeking unfrequented ground, for economic reasons as potent as those which send to similar areas well-to-do persons of cultivated taste, it may shed itself evenly over the whole island, converting it at last into one great suburban region diversified with national reservations of places of special beauty and interest, like Exmoor, the New Forest and the Lake District. Of course this is no prediction; predictors always leave out of account some contributing cause that has yet to show up; I merely indicate one of many possibilities, to show how uncertain is any one town's tenure of its status.

Consider the first few names of European cities of high fame and long descent that occur to the mind— Athens, Rome, Vienna, Paris, Florence, Ghent, Bruges, Augsburg, Lübeck. Is there more than one, in that handful of names, whose greatness time has not mauled? London herself has long suffered a decline in relative, though not in positive, size and importance. Until the nineteenth century opened, her primacy among British cities had hardly anything to match it in the world. It was like the place of Buenos Aires in the Argentine, or of Sydney in New South Wales. When the seventeenth century began, the second city of England, Bristol, had 30,000 people, but London had 500,000. In size, late mediaeval London was like a quite large modern town, a Portsmouth or Salford, set down in a country of villages, so soon had the rightly placed capital sucked the blood out of Winchester, York and every other possible rival. The twentieth century found London only five times as large as the next British city, instead of sixteen times. The Great Britain that once had contained a capital with half a million inhabitants and no other town with more than 30,000 had turned into a country with five million people in its capital, a million in each of three other cities, and an absolutely larger population within a thirty-five-mile radius from the centre of Manchester than within the same radius from Charing Cross. London had not been dethroned by the obsolescence of the original reasons of her greatness. And yet the change had told. At any rate the extraordinary new reasons for greatness in other places had altered the relative positions.

V

Regard the case of Liverpool, born a mud village in 1207. Even then nature had given her what is her fortune to-day. But it came in the form of a post-dated cheque; having it all the time in her pocket, she still could not cash it before the age of the large modern steamship. Her thirteenth-century fishing-boats sailed in and out of a harbour which nature's ingenuity had fitted already for Lusitanias and Olympics to use.

The Mersey estuary, as all children know, is bottle-shaped. The bottle's neck is between Liverpool and Birkenhead; the river is narrower there than at Aigburth or Garston, both farther inland. The port is one great natural pool, like a dock basin, with only a narrow way in. This has two happy effects. For one, the rise and fall of the tide within the pool is moderated. In estuaries like the Severn's or the Trent's the inrushing mass of the tide is pinched between two constantly converging banks. Crowded within a diminishing width of space, the advancing water heaps itself up on itself till you see such strange sights as the forty-foot rise of the Severn at a spring tide—the "bore," as it is called there—or the "aegir" that jostles its way up the Trent or the Firth of Solway. Into a bottle-shaped estuary less water can enter; when in, it stows itself without giving trouble; and when it goes out at the ebb it has to rush pretty fast through the neck of the bottle, so as to keep pace with the ebb of the sea outside. Twice a day this rapid seaward flow scours the narrow channel and keeps it deep. Twice a day the Mersey's mouth is dredged by nature. So, from a time when the infant Liverpool's shipping was coracles or canoes, the way was being made straight, gratis, for the liners that now lie in thirty feet of water a gangplank's length away from the Landing Stage.

Other causes helped. The port of Chester was disabled by the silting of the navigable channel of the Dee with sand which Chester had not the knowledge or energy to fight as Glasgow has fought and overcome the silt of the Clyde. Bristol was a tougher rival; but during the great naval wars Bristol, approached from the open sea, had not the snug security of Liverpool with her marine back entrance round the north of Ireland. Then came steam to redistribute industrial importance between the different parts of England. The rearrangement left Liverpool at the handle, as it were, of an open fan, with its ribs running out to a wide semicircle of great manufacturing towns, from Birmingham up to North-east Lancashire and the West Riding. Along every rib there poured down cargoes to load Liverpool ships. All England seemed to have been modelled to do Liverpool good—the Pennine arch heaved up and crushed and worn just so that the coal should crop out at the places whence it would bring freight to Liverpool ships; the Cheshire gap flattened out between the Pennine and the Cambrian hills just so that the first railways should find one of the only two easy routes to the north pointing from London to Liverpool.

Already the force of those causes is slackening. Scientific dredging is easier now. The depth of quay-side water that nature gave to Liverpool for nothing is got at Southampton without ruinous cost. Fears of foreign attack upon shipping have died down or taken new forms. A new redistribution of industrial importance between place and place would seem to have begun. But, whatever shadows be falling upon her, Liverpool still looks the part of the supremely fortunate port. Your spirits rise on seeing the Mersey just after high tide, with a brisk wind bickering against the swirling ebb in the channel by Seacombe, and all the river full of the incomparable glories of British and Scandinavian shipping. More stirring still, perhaps, to hear from the Wallasey shore the bellowing of the hooters and sirens of liner after liner coming in over the bar in a mild English winter twilight from the scorched ends of the earth. All the river side of Liverpool is quick with the visible drama of parting and of coming home. Without going to seek them you see the little huddled groups of numb emigrants from Eastern Europe, full of the immobile misery of thrashed horses, and the Irishman leaning out over the ship's rail, as she goes, to curse England. Here is the highly-coloured, sharply-accented life of a port; you sniff queer juxtapositions; a tonic curiosity aerates your mind and you feel as if you were travelling.

VI

The face of every town has its delicious differentness. What urban countenance is so amusingly demure as that of Stratford-on-Avon, with its set air of contained geniality, animated leisure, ordered complacency, everything with a note of reference in it to the auriferous Bard. For warmth give me red Knutsford: it glows like a firelit room full of old masters in heavy gilt frames; its mellow, settled habitableness the sum of all that men and women neither poor nor very rich could think of, in about nine hundred years, to make their town good to live in. Even Penrith, the windy little town of temperance inns, where trains take breath for a minute on their way to Scotland, and the cramped steep streets are full on Tuesday mornings of shambling, plunging cows and of tall blue-eyed men with lean reddish-brown faces—Penrith has a braced, hardy look of its own.

But of all cities, London, after all, is surely the finest to look at. You find it out if you have lived there in your youth, and then been long away, but sometimes revisit the place. You see it then with effectually opened eyes, as the man who has long been in some tropical wild sees rural England revealed while his train comes up from Plymouth through two hundred miles of trimmed, fenced garden, half-miraculous, half-laughable and wholly endearing. Fleet Street when the lamps are being lit on a clear evening; Southwark, its ramshackle wharves and mud foreshores, seen from Waterloo Bridge at five o'clock on a sunny June morning, the eighteenth-century bank of the river looking across to its nineteenth-century bank; the Temple's enclaves of peace where, the roar of the Strand comes so softened, you hear the lowest chirp of a sparrow, twenty yards away, planted clear and edgy, like a little foreground figure, on that dim background of sound; the liberal arc of a mighty circle of buildings massed above the Embankment, drawn upon the darkness in dotted lines of light, as a night train brings you in to Charing Cross; the long line of big ships dropping noiselessly down the silent river, past Greenwich and Grays, on the ebb of a midnight high tide—O, there are endless courses to this feast.

And it changes incessantly. Westminster Hall and the Abbey may give you a faint illusion of permanence, just as the Matterhorn does, though it is falling down into the valleys all day. But quit your London for some thirty years and then come back and look. Wych Street, un-widened since the Plague, has disappeared; Clare Market is gone, so is New Inn, the island church west of old Temple Bar is islanded now with a vengeance, right out in mid-stream, with the buses flowing all round it—it that used, like a

Thames ait, to hug the northern bank, with only a small back-water of roadway between; a little farther west along the Strand there has vanished that curious old constriction of a London artery, the pinched gut where the thud of the East-and-West traffic used to fall almost silent as all the horses slowed down to walk through the strait. And where is the old Globe Theatre, with its redolent name? And the Olympic, whose plaster and brick must surely have been all a-tingle with the quaint ingenuous tushery of "strong" Victorian drama, as old fiddles are with all the melody ever made on them? And, then the catacombish Opera Comique, into which your youthful feet would descend as into a mine, leaving behind the blessed light of day? What, "all my pretty ones?" Yea, and the old Strand Theatre too, on the south of the Strand, where "Our Boys" reigned in glory.

Yet it is all perfectly right. Let everything—almost everything—change with a will, in any city that you love. People gush and moan too much about the loss of ancient buildings of no special note— "landmarks" and "links with the past." In towns, as in human bodies, the only state of health is one of rapid wasting and repair. Wych Street, Clare Market, New Inn—they matter about as much as so many hairs or the tips of so many nails of some beloved person. The time for misgiving would come if the architectural tissues of London ever ceased to be swiftly dissolved and renewed. Woe unto her only when, like Ravenna or Venice, she buries no longer her architectural dead but keeps their bodies about her till they and she all mortify together into one great curio of petrifaction, like some antique mummy, a prodigy of embalmment. Kingsway, Aldwych and all the demolitions that made way for them were salutary signs of molecular activity in London's body. The Old Bailey was no bitter loss. Over Christ's Hospital itself the wise lover of London soon wiped away his tears. In the great ages of art, buildings have not been regarded as if immortality were their due. It is but an invalidish modern notion that any house which is handsome or has had an illustrious tenant ought to be coddled into the preternatural old age which the Struldbrugs of Gulliver found to be so disappointing. Cities whose health is robust are never content to live, as it were, on their funded capital of achievement in building or anything else; they push on; they think more of building well now than of not pulling down. And no cities are so excitingly beautiful as those in which architecture is still alive and at work, as it is in London to-day. Their faces are both ancient and young, without disharmony, for all good work, of any time or kind, can live at peace with the rest. The old looks and the young looks play a chequer-work over such faces; it may be as pleasant as any that patches of light and shadow make on the side of a hill on days of sunshine and blown cloud.

CHAPTER XIII

JOYS OF THE STREET

Within this hour it will be dinner-time:
Till that, I'll view the manners of the town,
Peruse the traders, gaze upon the buildings,
And then return, and sleep within mine inn.
Comedy of Errors, I. ii.

I

There are islands in the Pacific where one of your prime aims in life is not to be killed in your bed the next time your house is blown down by a hurricane. The hurricanes come at intervals of a few years; even earthquakes are quite on the cards; however your house may be built, it will have to come down. And so, when people build in those parts, they do not try to put up any cloud-capped towers or gorgeous palaces of stone; better far to have one side of a light match-box fall in on your head while you sleep than to have the most handsomely vaulted roof of massy marble or veined alabaster do the same thing. So the houses are built lightly of wood, the whole of each on one floor. If they have to be big, as a hospital has, they are made with a rich abundance of doors, so that, as soon as the air or the earth is smitten with frenzy, all the more helpless inmates can be swiftly carried out and laid down in the open.

As you would imagine, the architecture of places like this has a vivid eloquence of its own. To the reconnoitering eyes on every approaching ship it cries out the severe conditions on which life s retained in that island.

Other architecture may be less vociferous. But all architecture talks, and should talk, from the first to the last. The earliest Egyptian buildings speak freely about both sacred and secular things. We might have gathered from these informants alone, if we had not known it in other ways, that it was a very serious affair for an Egyptian, in his opinion, if his body were not left in a safe place after his death. When a man died, his soul, unless he had been good, was to go the round of various beasts, as a tenant of their several bodies. If he was good, his soul was to leave him for the time, spend three thousand years in the society of the divine Osiris and then come back to the same earthen tenement that it had quitted. Naturally an Egyptian architect, when he had to design a tomb, made sure that, whatever less practical grace it might lack, it would last out three thousand years good and so keep his client's embalmed body intact and fit for the soul to re-enter. Hence the fantastic solidity of a pyramid.

The chief secular thing that the greatest Egyptian architecture expressed was, I suppose, a primitive pride of conquest, cruel and vulgar. It seems that about the seventeenth century B.C. the rulers of Egypt became a somewhat Prussianistic set of believers in war as good business and not as a dire occasional necessity only. They went a-hunting their neighbours, brought back hordes of them, taken alive, and used them as slaves. They were such a supply of cheap labour as no kings, so far as we know, had ever had at their disposal before. The slave-raiding record was beaten and architecture had to commemorate the glorious performance. Clearly the most expressive way to do this was to build in such a fashion as nobody could have attempted who had not got the use of an unprecedented multitude of unpaid workmen. Hence a wanton massiveness of build, a swaggering amplitude of waste. It is the pride of all art, when in health, to take the simplest means to its ends. Here was an art, sick with pandering to sick souls, that has shown the world ever since how slight an achievement may be in proportion to all the toil that has gone to bring it off.

But some one may say: "Yes, architecture talks, and tells us interesting things—except in England, and now. We had an English architecture once. The men who built the cathedrals of Lincoln and Peterborough, Wells and Lichfield, had some sort of kinship, no doubt, in their art with the men who were building at Chartres, Amiens, Rheims and Rouen. But still they were English. Their buildings speak English, the English of their day. So does the work of our best painters and draughtsmen speak the English of to-day. But our architects! They seem to be like denationalised poets or painters who should set out to write a poem or paint a picture by saying to themselves: 'Now, shall I write this poem in the style of the Greek Anthology? Or of the Italian Renaissance? Or of the French Romantic epoch? ' Or 'Shall I paint this picture in the style of the Byzantines? Or of the Venetians? Or of the great Dutchmen?'

What expressiveness is there for us common Englishry in some accomplished person's scholarly exercises in Classical, Gothic, Palladian and other alien architectural styles?"

Well, there may be something in that. And yet the expressiveness of anything built to serve a human purpose, or that of a beaver or wren, is too eager to be easily gagged. You may travel after dark in winter through the textile counties in the north and know when you are entering a cotton-spinning region by the broad and lofty detached groups of hundreds of windows blazing with light, and when you pass into a weaving district by the wide, low expanses of sky-lighted sheds prone on the ground, their electric light showing dimly through the ground glass of their roofs. You may even tell by the relative sizes of those Aladdin's palaces, outlined on a ground of dark-ness by their own flare of brilliant windows, whether you are in a land of spinners of "fine counts," like Oldham, or "coarse counts," like Bolton. But by day every town in all the smutty Pleiades of English towns becomes an individual face, unlike every other and piquantly scored, as a human face is, with records of its life and marks of the labours or hobbies that have engrossed it.

II

Go to Liverpool or Manchester. Issue from your station of arrival and look about you. If you have only the commonplace well-to-do Englishman's eye that the standard education of his kind has dimmed, you may find the cities much alike. "Simply warehouses, everywhere," you may say, not knowing what rubbish you say. If by the grace of God or the help of a friend you have escaped mal-education, you will observe that in each city a warehouse means a different thing. The warehouses of Liverpool are huge strong-boxes of brick, aired and half-lit by a small number of windows and entered by the least gracious of practicable doors. Massive, sombre and grim, these buildings seem to disclaim airs and graces; they say "If you don't like our looks, keep away. We don't want you." And, since anything that a building says frankly and firmly has interest, no typical Liverpool warehouse is dull.

The typical Manchester warehouse says nothing like that. It has a welcoming entrance; its architect has designed this portal to exercise an inward suction, like the hospitable doors of inns and urbane private dwellings. Pains have clearly been taken to make all its rooms lightsome. Outside, it attempts, and often achieves, an air of dignity and a large unity. At its best it looks handsome and rich, but in a sober way, with composure and an impressive reserve.

These characters of brick and stone tell you that Liverpool is a place of transhipment and storage and Manchester a wholesale mart. The "big barrack warehouse" which the half-blind see everywhere in either city is in the one case a lock-up, in the other a show-room. And yet not a shop. In a Manchester textile warehouse things are being bought and sold all day, but not as in a shop. Both parties to every transaction are expert professionals. So catch-penny tricks are of no use. The vendor is like a barrister arguing before a judge sitting alone, and not to a jury. Nothing is here to be gained by the little dodges of window display that draw the poor impressionable amateur like you or me on to the premises of a hosier. All that wise building can do, within, to promote the business in hand is to admit the customer with a kind of stately geniality and then to make his movements about the interior easy, his light for examining goods abundant, and his impression of the firm's assured solidity profound. In the exterior it can give promise of those practical blessings within and it can especially express the reposeful solvency of the business, its ample reserves, its princely rank among merchants, its resolution to stay in the trade not for an age but for all time. Nothing of all this is needed to keep heavy merchandise dry and safe from thieves between its sojourns in a ship and in a train. So both kinds of warehouse are good. Both speak the truth about their intentions. But they are different and, to the ear that cares to listen to them both, such differences are delicious.

Leaving the warehouses, look at the banks. Every good bank is, at heart, like the first bank of all, the snugly defensible cave, with a stout stockade in its front, where a personable cave-man, club in hand, stood guard over the deposited flint treasures of the absent. It is a strong-room; it ought to look it; and it often does; there is in Mosley Street in Manchester a model of a great bank building, the work of Edward Walters, a local nineteenth-century architect as truly a master as the author of the modern theatre at Amiens. It makes you feel inclined to leave your money there, and all your plate too. It fills you with a sense of massive, world-defying security such as you get from the Strozzi Palace at Florence, and yet it is not lumbering; it has grace and the scholarship that we cannot do without now if we would; and beside it there sits, square and grave, a real modern town mansion.

Not, mind you, that diverting product of conflicting emotions, a country house in a town. Many Englishmen of wealth have built themselves country houses in town. Driven by custom or some ambition to live in London for part of the year, these Nimrods in exile have treated themselves to such aid as architectural genius could give them in dreaming they were not wholly cut off from the fox and the partridge. So, we suppose, there came into being such mansions as Crewe House, in Curzon Street— long and low and separated from the street by a kind of diminutive park, with a drive. They look like intended embodiments of unreason. They waste priceless land and they spoil the line of a street; and all, it would seem, to provide some spacious caterwauling-places for the region cats. Yet, viewed with the tenderness that can understand and forgive, they may express the poignant emotion of some broad-acred Squire Western dragged reluctantly to town for a few months; his womankind have done it, and the poor man languishes here for the views from his justice-room in distant Cheshire or Somerset. The late eighteenth-century novel and play tell of a species of civil warfare apparently endemic among the rural gentry; the wife and daughters ever and anon put up a fight for a seasonal descent upon the capital and all its social joys; the obdurate male vows that, for moral, aesthetic and financial reasons, nothing shall move him this year. "Budge," says the landowner's lady, with daughters to marry. "Budge not," says the landowner's heart; "stay with the game and the turnips, where you are safe." Some well-to-do couples, we may imagine, compromised on a sham country house in the capital.

Even now these mongrel habitations seem to inspire little shame in many of those who ought to know most of the points of a thoroughbred house. You will sometimes see "a country house in London" almost proudly advertised for sale by some eminent auctioneer who would think twice or three times before recommending to buyers "a town house in the New Forest." The true town house, like that I spoke of, is always contained, urbane and unfreakish. It frankly accepts the close propinquity of its fellows and bows to the necessity of more or less uniformity with them. It does not shirk, but delights in, the immediate contact of the street and the piquant interposition of only some inches of brick or a lamina of glass between the intimacies of the private life and public pavements where east winds are whirling straws and old rags of paper about in eddies of dust. Like any Palace over the Grand Canal, it overcomes triumphantly the severe conditions that it shall have only one facade to show, that three of its four sides shall be out of your sight and two of them blind. And if it be the official house of a banker it will look banker-like and nothing else. You may just remember the time when men of courtesy, on going into the bank where they kept their accounts, would take off their hats, the bank being still, to their sense, the parlour of a trusted professional friend and adviser whom they were calling upon. Indeed it almost was. Most banks were still private ones. Most bankers were still living over their banks. And the houses in which they both lived and did business expressed, when well built, not only the strength of a safe but the attributes of good sound men to bank with. Not grandiose or showy, but dignified in design and betraying no dismay at the cost of the best material, neither aping the abodes of "the quality" nor dissembling the possession of ample reserve funds, they fortified your faith that the head of Mr. Heywood was not to be easily turned, or that, whatever happened, Mr. Parr, at any rate, would never let you down.

III

As you go north from the centre of Oxford, along the wide boulevard of St. Giles and the Banbury or the Woodstock Road, you traverse, for several hundred yards of your walk, a region in which no one style of building prevails. There are houses that speak of the early nineteenth century, of the late and early eighteenth, and even of more distant dates. There are houses that seem, to this day, to be trying to save window-tax. There are a few huddled and cowering houses that look as if they had the weather or some other form of external menace much on their minds. And there are august and affable houses, like the old Judges' Lodging, consciously and securely the homes of people of consequence. "As I'm a person," old Lady Wishfort would swear, and, if such houses swore, their oaths would be like hers.

Out of this zone of diversity in age and in make you pass into a zone that wears a more uniform air. Here half the houses set you thinking of some Venetian Gothic fasade. The pointed arches over their porches murmur fondly of the thirteenth century. The windows of the servants' bedrooms are bisected vertically by little columns of marble. The conscientious constructor of wooden toy horses always strove "to come as near to Natur as I can for sixpence." So, to the sensitive eye and feeling heart, do these modern villas plead that under serious difficulties they are doing their best to resemble the Loredan Palace or the Ca'd' Oro or some other model of architectural virtue fronting the Grand Canal. This zone, as memory recalls it, is rather cold and grave in colour. It presents to your view many slates.

You emerge from it, almost abruptly, to enter a third zone. Here fealty is sworn to no Doges, but to Queen Anne. The whole quarter wears a warm flush. The walls are of a buxom red. Many roofs are red-tiled. Some of these roofs are of generous extent, their tops flouting the sky like Norwegian banners while their skirts offer to descend to the ground; they sometimes suggest that the architect's dearest wish was to let no man suffer from any shortage of box-rooms. Some of the chimneys are treated with much gusto and fancy; they must have given to their authors many amusing hours. Nearly all the woodwork is white; the whole colour scheme is the simple and chaste one seen in the Countess Olivia's face,

—whose red and white
Nature's own sweet and cunning hand laid on.

Remembering man's thrifty habit of building his habitation out of whatever material the soil presents on the spot, you may wonder, as you go on walking northward, whether, perhaps, some strange and serious geological "fault" has struck at right angles across the Banbury and Woodstock Roads. Can it be that a quarter or half a mile north of St. Giles's church the Oxford Clay of the geologists has abruptly come to an end and a bed of red sandstone has succeeded it in the position of top layer? Northerners, living on solid stone, have their houses stone-coloured; Notts and South Derbyshire men, children of the ruddy Keuper Marl, live in houses equally ruddy; Londoners, the nurslings of sundry new-fangled Eocene clays, acquiesce in a corresponding range of unsightly brick, extending from the turbidly purple to the wanly bilious. Here, in the neighbour-hood of Somerville College, do we, then, stand on one of the frontier cracks in the crust of the earth.

But, even while you muse, you pass out once more from zone into zone. In the new belt Queen Anne is indeed dead. Red brick is succeeded by greyish roughcast, or even by whitewash. The frames of windows sink in till they are flush with the walls. A conscious, conscientious plainness, a proud and rugged humility reigns. Here the Englishman's house is no longer entitled, like other castles, "Be voir" or "Norham" upon the front gate, but "The Croft," "The Shack" or "The Sheiling." The dignity of honest toil, the joy of plain living, the charm of "The Cottar's Saturday Night" and some other beautiful thoughts come into your mind as you traverse this zone of agreeable villas that make as if to escape in disguise as labourers' cottages.

Out beyond these are the open fields, waiting for yet other ripples of architectural invention or revival to break over them, sped outwards from the centre and power-house of aesthetic activity, somewhere in the neighbourhood of the Sheldonian and the Bodleian. Still, four sharply bordered zones are pretty good, to begin with. And these are as clear as the similar rings that you see in the sawn trunk of a tree, examined in section. Like those annular grainings they tell you a good many things, important or diverting. The grainings will tell you the age of the tree; they record what years of its life were lean and hard to live in, from want of rain or of sun; they keep a note of the time when some bad accident deranged the tree's growth, when it was half-starved by an extensive exposure of its roots or when some wholesale lopping of its upper branches left its trunk overstocked with sap for the year and set the stuff bursting out in a crowd of unnatural boughs low down on the stem. So the first slowly-grown ring of houses round Oxford expresses the great stretch of time for which the university, mediaeval and monastic still, created little or no need of genteel house-room outside its colleges and halls. The second ring, the ring of thronging villas tinged with Venetian Gothic art, expresses at once the new liberty given to Fellows to marry, the conscious, sensitive and slightly fashion-ridden culture of the first community of married Fellows and their wives, and the immense ascendancy of Ruskin over the educated minds of his time, especially the academic ones. The third, the Queen Anne ring, reports the mighty change of critical mode which followed. The yoke of Ruskin was thrown off; the taboo upon Renaissance and post-Renaissance architecture was denounced; the excess of dilettantism, affectation and pastiche in the less excellent work of the Gothic revival added force to a reaction which, anyhow, had to come, man being by nature unstable as water, not wholly to his disadvantage.

About the same time Oxford was becoming, socially, less isolated and autonomous, more an ordinary portion of middle-class England; many quite un-academic specimens of that England, indeed, were now using her as a Cheltenham or a Bedford, and filling the yard of her railway-station with shiny private carriages where there had once been nothing but the few and frowsy hansoms proper to poverty and learning. So suburban Oxford, in the second generation of the married don, fell easily in with the new architectural fashion then speckling the Surrey hills with the red bricks and tiles and bright white doors and window sashes of the Queen Anne style, as it was called, whatever a Queen Anne ghost might think of some of its gambols and fanfaronades. Then, in the due course of time, it became rather the exquisite note to be consciously poor. To be in the height of the fashion you had to be sorely stricken in purse by Mr. Lloyd George's notoriously depredatory taxes on land. At the same time, advanced liberal speculation was carrying part of the well-to-do classes into a mood of theoretic sympathy with the classes engaged in manual labour. So, from two directions at once, gentle winds of inspiration began to converge on the art of the architect. A magnified labourer's cottage, rough-cast and severe, could express either the indignant or the enthusiastic descent of the occupant from the exalted level of those who do not toil nor spin. You could live in a pleasant hovel so as to let it cry aloud to the world either "See what the Radical thieves have reduced me to," or "See the cross that I bear, out of my love for the poor." So easily and entertainingly may social history be studied in those gossipy pages, the fronts of suburban villas.

IV

No sort of weather, of course, can be dull anywhere—not even a great thaw—unless you have a dull mind to help it to bore you. But some sorts of weather are even more exciting than others. Most exciting of all, perhaps, in a city, are the first hours of romantic strangeness after a heavy fall of snow. While snow lies deep, the proportions of things are altered. Streets become much wider, especially if it be Sunday and not many people about. For the frontier between footpath and road is wiped out. Women look tallest in dresses with no horizontal lines of flounces or reefs round their skirts; in the same way a street widens out as soon as its width is not cut up into strips by the kerbs. Most city streets look much the better for this work of deletion. Their modern buildings commonly exceed in height the total width of roadway and footpaths. Thus they lose an element of handsomeness of which even the most squalid buildings cannot altogether deprive a broad street through a slum. Some part of this lost handsomeness returns when a deep coating of snow, still un-trodden, has made this surprising and charming addition to the width from house to house. It is as if every street had been improved, for good, by a miraculous setting back of the front on each side.

Another engaging and curious effect of snow in towns is the emphasis suddenly laid upon all visible roofs. Within a few minutes the upper part of a Gothic town-hall may become a system of steep hanging snow-slopes, like a Chamonix aiguille; they call out to be climbed or—it is much the same thing—to have their gradients considered. You may have never thought about city chimneys before: but now they present themselves to you in sharp black relief against those white sheets of snow-covered slate. They will not be denied. They appeal for fair play. They ask, have architects done chimneys justice? Or have they all this time been scornfully trusting the wretched lay citizen not to look up at any sky-line when he walks abroad?

Eye and mind are entertained and stirred by this abrupt and extensive redistribution of all the relative stresses that they have commonly laid on the component parts of a familiar scene. It imparts a piquancy akin to that which some well-known place may acquire when for the first time you look at it just after a clear midsummer sunrise, when all the long shadows are thrown in directions in which you have never seen them reaching out before. Of course buildings, in our climate, are not specially designed with a view to the figure that they will cut when well snowed upon. But then neither is a portrait in oils designed to be looked at upside down. And yet a painter sometimes finds it helpful to invert his canvas and see how it looks. In some such way it is not merely a lark, but a revelation or an exposure, to see how our familiar masterpieces of architecture look when the arbitrarily employed castor of the heavens has sprinkled capricious new accents on their several elements. They were not meant for such trials. Still they ought to be able to stand them.

Another pleasant freak played by snow upon modern cities, is to mediaevalise them—at any rate to illude you into the notion that it is doing so. Bond Street in London, or St. Ann's Square in Manchester, does not become, under snow, quite like the oldest parts of Chester or Tewkesbury. But the ordinary difference between them is immensely lessened. Is it that the more permanent elements in all domestic architecture are those which snow does least to mask, and that the contrast is strongest between just such orders of details as snow tends most to obliterate? Or is it only that in our habitual mental visions of mediaeval towns we are excessively inclined to imagine them snow laden because of the traditional fondness of popular historical romance and melodrama for "Christmas weather"—Jane Shore praying in the snow, among half-timbered, many-gabled dwellings, and so on? And that urban snow thus evokes in the common herd of us some semblance of a "residual mediaeval herd-consciousness," as the learned, or at any rate the polysyllabic, would say? Who knows? Perhaps every architect does, all the time. I only speak as an ignoramus, gazing at the splendid show that surrounds us on these great occasions.

V

Another time when cities are above themselves and shine with a kind of blithe novelty is when a lingering spring has softened at last and summer bursts like one bud, with a jubilant suddenness, seeming to spill its whole cornucopia of colour and fragrance on some one generous morning in June. Into the centre of cities it comes, not as it does to fortunate gardens, but with a kind of indirectness. It percolates. The glamour is refracted. Clerks come into town with home-grown flowers in their coats, as if by agreement; vases of roses fetched, all dewy, from suburban pleasaunces appear on the severe office tables of solicitors; genial modifications of attire give to the incoming morning tides at the great railway termini an innocently skittish air; the young man's awakening fancy issues in a frolic waistcoat, light in colour and weight; portly elders have got out their sportive white toppers again and feel they are cutting rather a dash: the spirit of the wanton lapwing is abroad. In the streets the early sunshine looks curiously kind; the air is still a little moist from the dawn, and all this radiant freshness seems to have a kind of compassion for yesterday's dust, thirsty luckless stuff that has lain all night in the streets and cannot even drink dew when it gets it. Birds in the trees of the Temple sing grace with a will for these surprising benefits, the care-worn plane-trees and elders in Wood Street, E.C., on the Embankment and in municipal tubs are visibly taking heart to tread the round of their embarrassed bodily functions once more; sparrows twitter from the eaves a new and braver simulation of the joy of psalmody in woods; the very corpse of summer fragrance, embalmed and stowed away in the perfumers' shops, confesses the influence of the season—life stirs again in those mummied essences, and the massed scents seem stronger when you pass the shop, as though on such a morning you were passing their native gardens at Grasse.

Thus the wonder and glory of the season come to you at one remove; you do not see the splendour of the June gardens and woods; you only infer them, you hear about them, you get at them through their effect on somebody else; they do not strike you directly but by ricochet action; they reach you filtered and qualified, passed through one or more of those interposed media, the plump city man and his less curvilinear clerk, the grimy town bird and the struggling town tree, and even the dust on the flags. Can it be just because of that, and not in spite of it, that these choice mornings in great towns have such a heart-searching loveliness? Consider the ways of skilled novelists. These, when they strive most to move you, do not try to bring you simply face to face with the places and people and actions that they describe. They do not just tell you that this or that happened at some charming place. They invent a character to interpose between you and the scene. They give you not the place itself, but the way it affected that character. They set that character to rave or stutter about it or just gape in front of it. Homer did not try to describe Helen's face. What he did was to say how the sight of it moved even elderly men. Thackeray draws no circumstantial portrait of Beatrix Esmond; he tells how everybody's head went round to look when she entered a box at the theatre. When Mr. Conrad has some glorious story to tell he does not tell it as coming from himself, a person knowing all; he tells us just how much of it attracted the interest of some far more commonplace person. Why? Because, by some subtle natural law, things come to us curiously enriched, in a certain way, when they come to us through an intervening observer or narrator. To whatever is attractive in the things themselves there is added the mysterious pleasure of deciphering the note taken of them by that actual or imaginary registrar. Mr. Kipling could have told the story of his "Love o' Women" much more fully if he had told it as an omniscient author—all authors, of course, are omniscient about their inventions. And yet he knew that he could charm us more by giving it as told by a rather ignorant and half-understanding private soldier. Is there some kinship, perhaps, between the fine little psychological law which applies in that case and the curious refinement of power that summer may have to move us in cities? For here it comes, not straight and whole but, as it were, narrated piecemeal and lamely by divers fragmentary reporters. Through her influence on pursy cit and modish spark, through her power of animating grimy sparrows and plane-trees, the Lady Flora comes to us a creature of inference and mystery, even more exciting perhaps to curiosity and the creative imagination than the goddess whom we see full face, walking in all her furbelows and flounces among the flower-beds at Hampton Court and down the glades of Kew.

VI

We all see more of architecture than of any other art. Every street is a gallery of architects' work, and in most streets, whatever their age, there is good work and bad. Through these amusing shows many of us walk unperceivingly, all our days, like illiterates in a library, so richly does the fashionable education provide us with blind sides. And yet the alphabet of building is not desperately hard to learn. To make out, more or less, what a builder has tried for, how his site and surroundings have helped him or stood in his way, what means he has chosen to take to his end, out of all those that the experience of other builders has left him to choose from, what kind of stuff he has built his house of, and how far he has gone to get it—all these, when once you begin, may become almost exciting subjects of speculation, without being toilfully abstruse.

The uttermost charm of a building, however, can only be got at by practising a certain shifting of your mental position, a kind of lift or displacement that shows things to you from an unaccustomed side. Every one has felt the quaint naivety of primitive buildings. They affect us like the grand contrivances of children, their cave dwellings and tree houses which touch and amuse us with their contrast between the small creatures' great notions and their little powers. This savour is almost equally strong in ancient houses that still stand, with their eager, hampered attempts to attain some ingenuous ideal of snugness, well out of the rain, and in the wigwams and kraals of those of us who are still savages. You find it afresh wherever people are thrown out, as it were, naken on the earth again, to tend for themselves from the beginning. See the infant architecture of dug-outs in war, and of shacks that men, left to live in houseless wastes, immediately begin to make of biscuit-tins and old soap-boxes. They reek with this touching interest of the weak, contriving little animal struggling like ants or a beaver set down in a strange and bad place to get things going decently around him. How cunningly he sheathes the wet south-western wall with rags of old tin! And how on earth will he manage the chimney? Pitifully short of tools, materials, time and knowledge, the dauntless creatures toil and blunder on in pursuit of some vision of their own; we view their handiwork long afterwards with something like the curiosity and tenderness of mothers examining their sleeping children's vast enterprises of building in sand.
As surely as an ancient cottage possesses that moving quaintness for us, so surely will our buildings of to-day have some of it as soon as a few centuries have made part of our mechanical difficulties obsolete and shown some of our methods to be circuitous means to simple ends. Buildings that people will treasure for their quaintness in five hundred years are going up to-day; and Kingsway, perhaps, is founding a rude picturesque ancientry which people will go to see as they go now to walk on the walls of Conway and to see the Chester Rows. Why should we not achieve some transportation of ourselves, in thought, to the point from which these unborn spectators will see our offices and homes? The thing is

feasible. It has been done. Charles Lamb could go about the London of his day with just that pensive, penetrative sense of the curious human expressiveness of the place which we feel in the Old Town at Edinburgh, or in Ravenna. With an affection only less poignant than that of mothers, who can sometimes see already in their new-born infants the greyness and the wrinkles that will come, Lamb could anticipate in imagination the gradual deposits of time and see his contemporary London with all the emotional creepers already clinging about it which seem to ourselves to have grown since he died. If we can only do that, no modern street will be dull and the rawest new house may have already something of the fascination that it will assuredly have if it stands till the year 3000.

At any rate a little sympathy will disengage from a new building its indestructible interest as a contrivance, and a term in a long series of contrivances, every term in the series becoming rather winningly childlike as soon as a few more terms have followed it. Little effort is needed to see that childlike quality persisting on into the very term that is reached to-day and to find, perhaps, in walls of steel and concrete not so much a final perfection of cunning as a brave little effort to make shift with such means as we have, till the real thing comes. Faulty design, even vulgarity, may have its freakish interest. Some eighteenth-century chateaux in the north of France are only one room thick from back to front, to their apparent magnification, though much to the refrigeration of the occupants. Their avenues, too, may have the trees wider apart at one end than at the other, to gain a false effect of length. The droll little snobs! You really cannot be angry with humbugs so infantine. Caddishness itself, when grown into an antique, becomes a curio rather than an offence. And so some charity may well be practised, to one's own profit, in viewing even those fruits of the fancy of speculative builders, the painty red suburban villas that seem to affect a likeness to ordinary houses lightly shelled with field-guns and then glazed at the holes, so that a little window of a funny shape may be found over the chimney-piece or in a corner of a room. If one of them were to live for a thousand years, how much the people of that age would be amused by seeing it! And why not enjoy that amusement ourselves?

CHAPTER XIV

WHAT IT ALL COMES TO

All places that the eye of Heaven visits
Are to the wise man ports and happy havens.
Richard II., I. iii.

I

The quest of the right place is over, without a mark left on the map to show that the right place is there. It seemed for a time to be high on the Alps, and then down by a lake at their feet, or else beside the Adriatic sands, or under Picardy poplars, or among Tuscan or Umbrian walnuts and vines. Thence it shifted its site to our own less illustrious rivers and hills, and then to one of the least richly storied of the roads that cross them, and so to the average house you see behind the roadside trees, and at last to the workaday streets of towns that incur, with their plain faces, the censure of distinguished critics. Where, then, does rightness abide? How recognise it at sight, and make for it straight, shaking off from our boots the dust of places wrong or indifferent?

But another question comes first. What is a place—any place? Is it really that constant, precisely definable thing that our common uses of the word would seem to imply? Amid much that was vague in our sensations and unstable in our thoughts, space and time used to appear to stand fast, as the fixed stars did in those times. They seemed, like these, to hold out for our reassurance or reproof a standard of unquestionable fact, or of unalterable law. But of late Time himself has been losing some part of his reputation for an inexorable precision and firmness. Science has shown us the same event—the passing of a comet, perhaps, or the bursting of a distant star—visible at one moment in its own neighbourhood and visible at a later minute, hour, or day at some point more remote. Our minds are set toying with new fancies. Suppose that a creature having human sight and hearing, but of a power and fineness immensely increased, could travel indefinitely far away from the earth, and travel faster than rays or vibrations of light travel through space. After going some millions of miles he would overtake waves that had been sent journeying into the void by yesterday's physical occurrences upon the earth. He might look back and see a man still living who died, as we on earth would say, last night. As the traveller went further away, time would continue to run its course backwards: the rolled-up scroll of history would unroll itself again; the cheers that rose from London streets at the Restoration might presently come into hearing, and bonfires twinkle into sight again that were lit by Norman soldiers at Hastings the night after Harold was killed. In a sense Caesar is still being slain in the Capitol, and Hannibal struggling over the Alps, and Horatius defending the bridge, if indeed he ever did any such thing. Perhaps it may only be said that these things are past in so far as the person who says it happens to stand at one point in the physical universe rather than another.

Space, with its seemingly concrete filling of solids and liquids and gases, soon loses a part of its fixity too. It stands or falls with time, for each can only be stated in terms of the other. If you or I were God, and had the power of ubiquity that is commonly ascribed to God, we should be at the same time close to this earth and also at immense interstellar distances from it. The reach of our sight and hearing would not have limitations, as now. Thus we should see with the same eye at the same moment the world's events of to-day and also those of all past ages, as we call them, near and remote, all going on. The illusion of time would vanish. But something of space would go too. For in our sight a turfy down of chalk would still run from Dover across to Boulogne; and a greater Rhine, with the Trent and the Ouse for tributary streams, would still be flowing northward through meadows which—as seen from less far off—we call the North Sea. And yet the North Sea would be visibly lying there too. More subversive still, we should see, from our various, but simultaneous, posts of observation, the verdant earth of to-day and, filling the same position, a whirl of flaming gases twisted by their own movement into a fiery ball. Two un-mistakably different things would at the same moment be visibly occupying the same space. Poor old Time! Poor old Space!

All that most of us can know about any place, or portion of space, that we pass through is that it stirs in us some emotion or other, which we have no means of comparing closely with any emotion that it may stir in any one else. The moment that we attempt to describe it, we offer something which may be descriptive of it, but is more certainly descriptive of ourselves. Hardy's Wessex is only a slightly indirect portrait of Hardy; the Venice of Ruskin may not be found in the Adriatic by all, but in it all may see Ruskin drawn to the life. We are prone to talk as if some place, or some work of art, that is famous for its beauty were always the same thing, a certain fixed treasure to which anybody can go at any time, and in any state of himself, and still find it there. But many things must have happened in the inside of yourself before even the most celebrated of these cynosures can make much difference to you—and you are the only person for whom you can ever know for certain how much the difference amounts to. A dimness in your eyes or an ache in your stomach is only one out of countless variations through which Taormina or Vallombrosa passes according to the several bodily and mental states and equipments of those who—as we say in a rough, general way—"see" it. Say, if you choose, that you collaborate with the place to create its full beauty; or say that this beauty is a relation between the place and yourself; or that, as some philosophers say, the place is you—although this last seems to most of us difficult. At any rate you are deeply involved in the authorship of the net effect on your mind. "Silly old washerwoman, she and her brat," I have heard a very good fellow say at sight of the Sistine Madonna. Here the collaborators, my friend and Raphael, seem to have hardly succeeded at all. "What I don't like in mountains," another good fellow has told me, while we stood at the heart of the Snowdon range and he ruefully viewed its wide expanses of bare rock, bilberry and heather, "is all this' here plain stuff. There's a lot o' plain stuff between Capel Curig and here." Again that imperfect success in joint authorship.

II

Between our senses and any object that might stir us to some genial or aweful delight there is always interposed a kind of ether distilled from our own personality. All that can ever come to us must come in such vibrations as that intervening medium can suffer to pass. We never really get at the object itself; what we get is always some highly personal sense of the object, a sense strongly coloured and flavoured by ourselves, our temperament's particular quality of reaction under whatever stimulus the object may exert.

To the artist who knows his business this is a common-place. It is the point that he starts from, to paint a landscape, or even a portrait. He renounces any attempt to represent things as an impersonal science might describe them. He does not care, either, to represent in paint a kind of greatest common measure of what a large number of other persons might be conjectured to see in the object before him. He aims at expressing, with the most intimate frankness, whatever is most uncommon and vehement, perhaps most wayward and fantastic, in his private enjoyment of such visions as arise in his own mind when thrilled by its own delighted reaction to the things in question. As I have said elsewhere, "to mix with the day's diet of sights and sounds the man of this type seems to bring a wine of his own that lights a fire in his blood as he sits at the meal. What the finest minds of other types eschew he does, and takes pains to do. To shun the dry light, to drench all he sees with himself, his own temperament, the humours of his own moods—this is not his dread but his wish, as well as his bent. 'The eye sees what the eye brings the means of seeing 'A fool sees not the same tree that a wise man sees 'You shall see the world in a grain of sand, and heaven in a wild flower'; this heightened and delighted personal sense of fact, a knack of seeing visions at the instance of seen things, is the basis of all art."

We humbler bodies cannot do all that. And yet, in some slight measure, every man must be his own artist; since he is fated to get, in any case, only some qualified visions of places and other things, he may as well take thought in time to get his visions as fresh and as un-deformed as may be. None of us can force the divine accident to happen, or make ourselves see all that Milton saw in the climbing of the twilight sky by the first lark at an English midsummer dawn. And yet none of us knows but that one of these tremendous annunciations may come at any moment to himself. Two things, at any rate, he can do. The first is to keep clean the lens on which any vision that comes shall be printed. The second is to make sure that the lens is his own.

III

This is no tract upon morals. It is a handbook to pleasures. But morals make up such a big part of life that you cannot talk long about anything else without finding that, here too, some matter of conduct comes in. So out with it straight and on with our business.

There is a notion, common among hobbledehoys, that "experience" can be widened by a loss of self-control. Some of them will misbehave themselves just to "see life." Diddled by stale figures of speech, a lad at the university will get drunk "just to have the experience," or do something worse because he wants to have "experienced everything" or to "know the whole of life." And some half-sane or trashy-hearted writers of fuller age have erected this mess of vague thought into a kind of philosophy. Life they regard as an opportunity for collectorship, and they think of any new thing, noble or foul, that one does or sees as an addition to one's collection and an enrichment of one's personality; it makes one's life, they fancy, fuller and more complete, more richly hung with notable pictures; it enlarges a man's knowledge of his own soul and helps him to gain a deeper insight into the heart and meaning of the whole world. It is said that Oscar Wilde, when slowly dying of a retributive disease, with all his splendid gifts already dead before his body, was still chattering about the amplitude of the career of moral un-control.

These ethics of the dust rest wholly on one blunder. They assume that every novel step which you take must needs increase your experience and not diminish it. Their algebra of experience recognises only the positive sign. They reckon with no minus experiences. They think of the clean boy who gives up his cleanness as if he had added something to his experience and subtracted nothing; whereas, at every loss of self-control, you make some exchange of the spacious lightsome experience of moral autonomy for the dark and narrow experience of moral helplessness: you always come off a net loser, your treasury of experience depleted on balance, your vision of life more or less blurred, your register of experience smudged, your faculty for delight perceptibly enfeebled. Burns had tried the thing out; he knew all about it when he wrote, of un-control,

It hardens all within
And petrifies the feeling.

He and a few other possessors of genius have done some wonderful things though they lived, off and on, in the sensual sty, and died in it. Marlowe and Morland and Burns and Mangan and Wilde, all had time, before they quenched their own light, to show what their continued splendour might have been. But that makes out no case for self-destruction. And, short of total self-destruction, you cannot defile the temple without dimming its windows. Defile it much and your experience of life may dwindle down to a mere pin-point, all sensation and vision and memory contracting, as it does in shattered rakes, to the sense of the prick of one joyless craving that frustrated all its hopes of satisfaction long ago. Defile it only a little, and something is lost already of the radiant receptiveness of the delighted spirit with no ugly secrets to keep. It was no random wording that made the "seeing" of God the special beatitude of the pure in heart, or that gave the gift of a transfiguring vision to "minds innocent and quiet" in the great Cavalier's poem. The man "who is not passion's slave" wins more than the love of Hamlet. A quick and lightsome alertness waits at the side of his bed every morning, to enter into his senses as soon as he wakes. "Get up," it says, "you have great things to see to-day." Perhaps the weather has changed in the night, and he experiences a chuckling glee as if the everlastingly amusing changefulness of weather had never struck him before. All these ancient marvels come to him again with an unexhausted freshness; the sun is up, shining on be-jewelled grass; it is all old beyond words and yet it is great news.

Unconsciously he gives the thanks that consists in infinite silent contentment and sings the hymn of a blithe wonder at wonder's own indefeasible freshness:

Thou dost preserve the stars from wrong,
And the eternal heavens through thee are fresh and strong.

Whew! This talking of morals is pretty hot work for one who has less of Wordsworth or of Ecclesiastes about him than of a monkey much given to jumping about on the trees of our Paradise. Still, the thing forced itself in; even the monkeys have to keep fit in order to get the best out of their jumping.

IV

Well, suppose we have no deadly sins, nor even some wary and sly little vices to keep our eyes turned in, instead of out, when we get up of a morning. Still we may have much to do, or undo, before the old veil can lift and full vision be ours. For not in morals alone but in this shy demesne of aesthetics as well is it the bare truth that unless you become as a little child, or have not ceased to be one, the best that there is to be had will not come your way.

You can hardly mistake the fortunate few who have not lost the finer use of their eyes—their bodily and mental eyes together—as most of us do in the later stages of youth. The lucky ones—most of them some sort of artists, but not by any means all—seem to be always as if they had just come into the world and were going over this remarkable find, in a delectable state of wonder or amusement. There is still in them something of Adam upon the first day: they reconnoitre, with shining eyes, the lay-out of the garden, and stare in admiration at such novel curiosities as the moon and stars. They seem to be always in at the birth of these remarkable things, unlike the rest of us, who take Orion and the Great Dog pretty calmly, as belonging to rather an old story and one which no archaic fashion is trying at the moment to revive. You can make out that some of them see their human surroundings, the life and customs of their time, with that affectionate sense of its characteristic manner and colour which most of us can only bring to the study of some specially picturesque period, and then only if this has been much written up by engaging authors: twentieth-century London or Glasgow is quaint and picturesque to them now as Dr. Johnson's London, or the old St. Albans, is to common persons of taste. Our rather weary, faded habit of thinking only of splendid traditions as things that originated long ago, is not theirs; they exult in traditions that men are founding to-day, and count it better to have a part in the making of what may be storied and immemorial foundations two thousand years hence than to bask in the sunshine of fond reverie in which we see Oxford or Winchester swimming like lovely landscapes enveloped in haze. Or the fumes of mere human fellowship go to their heads, as if no cant or rhetoric had ever come to lower the strength of those generous strong waters I know not how far below proof; and these eccentrics actually feel as if man were naturally united to man by the bond uniting a boatload of sailors newly cast away on a small uninhabited island. Many will even act accordingly.

Not so much as a notion of any such state of the mind can be passed on to anybody to whom the state itself is utterly alien. But nearly every one's experience includes some inkling of it: one of the winds that blow as they list has blown our way and brought us at least some fugitive glimpse of the things that we might still be seeing if nothing had stepped in to take away from us the power of sight that we once had. Perhaps what passes for a thoroughly first-rate education has done the blinding. This may have brought us to think that it is freakish, or even ill-bred, to see things for ourselves and enjoy them with vehemence. A child's mind is unconsciously autonomous, its way of observation boldly individual, its expression eagerly original. "Lamps o' beauty, lamps o' beauty," I have heard a small child crooning to itself as it watched some blown daffodils swinging in the twilight. Another, on first noticing a mounting lark, said "Look—two wings tied together, and a little bit of stick, which is its beak!" That is how the undespoiled see and describe, the delighted perception rushing straight into live speech that cares for no canons and yet shirks no flight. But presently this wild gusto and grace are tabooed by the joint efforts of elder comrades and of the many second-rate minds to be found among teachers, along with the few that fire and guide and hearten: the little adventurer's heart is prevailed on to fail him; he gives up his treasure of insight and power; within a few terms he may come to talk and think, and even to see, as imitatively and timidly as a committee: stock jokes, stock phrases, stock valuations, stock contempts —he is more or less forcibly fed with them, till he imbibes at last a sense of actual discomfort and distrust, instead of admiration, in the company of any one who does not see and hear by proxy and talk by rote. He has been turned, for life, into a member of a set, a creature of dim vision and savourless speech and nervous conformities. And yet he may, like the caged larks, have his moments of imaginative release into that old state of himself when no screens were put up between him and the sun. At some emotional crisis, or some propitious moment of travel, a break in the long doldrums may come and the immobilised sails may seem for an instant to feel a breeze rise as it used to do.

V

All that any one else can helpfully say to that poor fellow is only this commonplace: "Give all your sails to the wind. Trust to your own native sense of the object before you; let it abound in its difference from anything that you have heard worshipful persons describe as appropriate feelings in some similar case."

The assumption is commonly made, or implied, that in presence of some reputedly beautiful thing there is one right way of feeling, or thinking, and that there are many wrong ways. The opposite is the truth. No wrong way exists, so long as it is a vehement personal way of somebody's own. Any such human experience is the ultimate unit of critical truth; you cannot get higher authority than that sincere assurance for any valuation of any visible thing. The only way you can fail, as a spectator of nature or art, is to say things, and try to believe them, just because some aesthetic pundit or critical mandarin has said them before. That way humbug lies, and boredom too.

And yet, strait and narrow is the way. For that which one's elders say is often worth minding. You look at Botticelli's "Judith" with wiser eyes if you have read the clash of golden and silvery words in which Ruskin ascribes to her one state of feeling and Pater another. You look from Richmond Hill a better man, for the purpose in hand, if you know already how that great prospect moved Turner and how it moved Scott. Only, beware of them all. Hear what they say: "take each man's censure"; but always "reserve your judgement," and let it never be formed by the poor canny self-protective process of thinking out first what judgement would sound best from our lips, or would look least cranky if read, and then forcing ourselves towards that. Why not, each of us, have the courage of our own sensations and face the facts of our own likings and dislikes. It does not really matter if they bring on us the scorn of either the "superior person" or the "man of the world," the two alternative bogeys that, between them, scare so many people out of all faith in their own honest preferences and enjoyments.

Only, I fancy, through this sort of jealously guarded home-rule are the great appreciations of beauty achieved. Most of us, of course, will never achieve anything great of that kind; we shall not feel as much as Ruskin felt at sight of St. Mark's, or Meredith when he watched from Venice the first sun striking the Alps. Still, if we cannot achieve a big thing, we can at least achieve a real one. Some passionate moment of admiration verging on adoration may come—the intense and glowing sense of an admittance, a new insight gained, not copied nor vamped but irresistibly experienced, like sunlight or growth. So, in this work of enjoying let us acknowledge no oracles or suzerains; every one fend for himself, and then something worth having may come of it; for on no other terms will it come.

VI

So it works round to this—the delights of one place or another reside rather more in ourselves than they do in the place. The Alps at after-glow may be made trite and dull by some failure of ours to master a mean little fear or desire; the finest fairy-tale that Nature ever told may come to nothing more than a lifeless humming in your ears if you see a lot of her other children not minding it and have not learnt to do your own listening for yourself. All the details of our own state affect, in some little measure at least, the quality of things that we see and even of things that we saw long ago. To many English exiles long in the tropics, well branded and drenched with years of the extravagant unfriendliness of soddening rains and skies of hard, hot tin, there comes a boundless increase in the beauty of the common English country town that they see in their thoughts. Its friendly glow, its air of reasonable contentment, of order temperately kept, and of unflustered diligence, the slowly-printed record of many generations of cheerful and good-natured people, easy to understand and to live with—these things come by their rights; they establish more fully than ever before the claims of their beauty. A long-familiar country house or farm that you remember flushing to heart-warming reds in the horizontal light of the endless English summer evening, the longest and kindest in the world, or standing up out of low meadow mists in the primeval-seeming stillness of late afternoon in the grave October weather when fires in deep hearths begin to grow wonderful—this is not just one good-looking thing, but a long scale of things ascending from dreary plainness to the loveliness that makes your small heart ache with over-filling; and some state of oneself, not of anything else, is registered by the place where it seems to stand on the scale. It may be to you the occasion of some vision as trivial and poor as a bilious man's vision of food, or a vision all on fire with heart-rending beauty and truth, like the one a man gets of the life of his mother when she has just died.

Away, then, with the critical pertness that classes one place as sufficiently fair to be loved and sets another place aside as unsightly. It has been airily said, in our time, that Sheffield and even London are ugly. London! London on an early autumn afternoon of quiet sunshine, when all the air is mysterious with a vaporous gold-dust of illuminated motes and the hum of the traffic seems to fall pensive and muted round the big, benign London policeman with uplifted hand Conducting the orchestral Strand.

London ugly! Or Leeds not an Athens! Or Birmingham not the right place! Just look at them all, with your own mind and body decently fit, and your feelers well out and your retina burnished. For all places, when properly looked at, illuminate or set off one another: they do not fight for crowns of beauty in your esteem; members one of another, while ministering also to your sense of effective contrast, they join to lead you on towards conscious possessorship of your whole visible world as a single estate, wholly yours now and the whole of it always implied in any one of its parts that you may happen to see. Attain to that and you carry the centre of things about in your mind, and the right place is wherever you are.

Charles Edward Montague was born in London on New Year's Day, 1867.

Montague was the son of Francis Montague, an Irish Roman Catholic priest from County Tyrone, Ireland, who after falling in love with Rosa McCabe, the daughter of a successful merchant from Drogheda, left the Church, married Rosa and, in 1863, moved to England.

His education was excellent; he attended the City of London School and then went on to university at Balliol College, Oxford.

Whilst at Oxford he achieved, in 1887, a First in Classical Moderations and two years later a Second in Literae Humaniores.

In addition to his time studying Montague, a keen writer, wrote several and well-respected literary reviews for the Manchester Guardian.

In February, 1890, the editor, C. P. Scott, invited him to Manchester for a month's trial at the paper. Montague was obviously an impressive young man and he was soon given a full-time job.

It was here that Montague was to begin his career in earnest; his hard work and talents turning him into a respected leader writer as well as drama critic.

Montague and Scott shared the same political views and between them they turned the Manchester Guardian into a vibrant and campaigning newspaper. Today it would be called a mission statement back then it was stated as "to bring all political action to the same tests as personal conduct".

This quickly led to their support of Irish Home Rule, a divisive issue at the time. Scott was now to take his views in front of the public and stand for Parliament. He was elected to serve between 1895 and 1906 and Montague now became the de facto editor of the paper. Once more the paper ran contrary to government policy and was in opposition to the Boer War which had begun to show many of the latent evils that war was to bring in terms of its brutalising conduct and the use of new technology and new ideas.

The relationship between Montague and Scott also became one of father and son-in-law when Montague married Scott's only daughter, Madeline, at the Unitarian Chapel in Manchester in 1898.

Montague had always had a great interest in literature and theatre and by the turn of the century was applauded as one of England's leading drama critics. Such was their insight and popularity that many of these essays were gathered together and later printed in book form.

As the storm clouds of war gathered over Europe in the summer of 1914 both Montague and Scott argued in the paper against Britain becoming involved in a war on the continent.

However argument was futile. When the Arch Duke was shot the dominos fell one after another. Britain intervened and went to the aid of its Allies. The First World War was now upon them with all its savagery and butchery.

Montague believed that it was important to give full and unequivocal support to the British government now that war was upon the Country. The general feeling that 'it will be all over by Christmas' became a realisation that it would drag on for years and the world now watched the horrific spectacle of trench warfare where tens of thousands were slaughtered for an advance of a few yards.

Montague wrote to Scott: "I have felt for some time, and especially since I have been writing leaders urging people to enlist, a strong wish to do the same myself. I wrote last week to the War Office to ask if there was any chance of getting over the difficulty of my few years over the limit of age, and I was told that although the War Office could not directly break the rule itself, it did not veto exceptions made by those responsible for the raising of new battalions locally."

Those 'few years' were, in fact, decades. Montague was now age forty-seven with a wife and seven children dependent upon him. Although his hair had been grey since his mid-twenties, he made a passable attempt at dying it darker in order to help persuade the army to take him. (or, as H. W. Nevinson put it in his witty and truthful way "Montague is the only man I know whose white hair in a single night turned dark through courage.") On 23rd December, 1914, the Royal Fusiliers accepted him and he joined the Sportsman's Battalion.

His military training was held at Climpson Camp in Nottingham. By November, 1915, Montague had been sent to France.

Upon his arrival on the Western Front, his commanding officer at once questioned the wisdom of having a man in his late forties in the trenches. Montague was sent before the Medical Board on 28th January 1916. He wrote "I went in and found the Colonel-Surgeon, who had barred me a month ago on the ground of my age, again presiding. He looked up at me genially, when I came to the table, and said, "So I hear you want to have another whack of the Germans". I admitted that I did. "How old are you - I mean, your real age?" "Forty-nine, Sir", said I, "but only just". "Sure you're fit?" I said yes. Another doctor at the table said something about my having been there before. "Yes, yes", said the Colonel, "I remember him perfectly. Well, Sergeant, all right", and he marked me a big 'A' on his report. I grinned and saluted and made off. He called after me as I was making for the door, "Sergeant, I believe you'll do better up there than some of the young uns".

Whatever the virtues of his patriotism it did help to bring about a new rule. Three months later it was announced that all men over forty four were to be banned from trench work.

Being a soldier in the trenches was hell on earth. You were either fighting, being shelled by artillery or living cheek by jowl in deep, muddy slits of earth where conditions can only best be described as appalling, the landscape often littered with dead and rotting corpses.

Montague wrote of the conditions to Francis Dodd: "The one thing of which no description given in England any true measure is the universal, ubiquitous muckiness of the whole front. One could hardly have imagined anybody as muddy as everybody is. The rats are pretty well unimaginable too, and, wherever you are, if you have any grub about you that they like, they eat straight through your clothes or haversack to get at it as soon as you are asleep. I had some crumbs of army biscuit in a little calico bag in a greatcoat pocket, and when I awoke they had eaten a big hole through the coat from outside and pulled the bag through it, as if they thought the bag would be useful to carry away the stuff in. But they don't actually try to eat live humans."

The journalist, Philip Gibbs, later recalled: "Prematurely white-haired, he had dyed it when the war began and had enlisted in the ranks. He became a sergeant and then was dragged out of his battalion, made a captain, and appointed as censor to our little group. Extremely courteous, abominably brave - he liked being under shell fire - and a ready smile in his very blue eyes, he seemed unguarded and open. Once he told me that he had declared a kind of moratorium on Christian ethics during the war. It was impossible, he said, to reconcile war with the Christian ideal, but it was necessary to get on with its killing. One could get back to first principles afterwards, and resume one's ideals when the job had been done."

Montague was, as described earlier, a worker, a doer, and was soon promoted to the rank of second lieutenant and with it a transfer to Military Intelligence. For the next two years he had the task of writing propaganda for the British Army and censoring articles written by the five English journalists authorized to write, albeit with 'help' from the censor, on the Western Front.

Another of his duties was to escort important visitors for tours of the trenches. Among his charges were: David Lloyd George, Georges Clemenceau, George Bernard Shaw and H. G. Wells. (It is a bizarre thought now that this could happen but just over 60 years earlier many had picnicked with their wives on the hill-tops as the various battles of the Crimea war unfolded in the valleys below).

But the carnage also re-kindled his own feelings that War in the end solves little. Disillusioned by its scale, futility and bleak prognosis, he wrote a note in his diary in December 1917: "To take part in war cannot, I think, be squared with Christianity. So far the Quakers are right. But I am more sure of my duty of trying to win the war than I am that Christ was right in every part of all that he said, though no one has ever said so much that was right as he did. Therefore I will try, as far as my part goes, to win the war, not pretending meanwhile that I am obeying Christ, and after the war I will try harder than I did before to obey him in all the things in which I am sure he was right. Meanwhile may God give me credit for not seeking to be deceived."

George Bernard Shaw was one of those who Montague took for a tour of the frontline trenches: "At the chateau where the Army entertained the rather mixed lot who were classified as Distinguished Visitors, I met Montague. Finding him just the sort of man I like and get on with, I was glad to learn that he was to be my leader on my excursions. The standing joke about Montague was his craze for being under fire, and his tendency to lead the distinguished visitors, who did not necessarily share this taste into warm corners. Like most standing jokes it was inaccurate, but had something in it.... Both of us felt that, being there, we were wasting our time when we were not within range of the guns. We had come to the theatre to see the play, not to enjoy the intervals between the acts like fashionable people at the opera."

In November 1918 the war was over and Montague could now return home to his wife and family and also to the Manchester Guardian where he would continue to stay until retirement in 1925.

After the end of World War I Montague wrote in a strong anti-war vein; "War hath no fury like a non-combatant." Disenchantment (written in 1922), a collection of newspaper articles about the war, was one of the first prose works to strongly criticise the way the war was fought, and is a pivotal text in the development of literature about the First World War. Disenchantment criticised the British Press' coverage of the war and the conduct of the British generals. Montague accused the latter of being influenced by the "public school ethos" which he condemned as a "gallant robust contempt for "swats" and for all who invented new means to new ends and who trained and used their brains with a will".

Perhaps the paragraph in Disenchantment that most readily captures his overall feeling is: "The freedom of Europe, The war to end war, The overthrow of militarism, The cause of civilization - most people believe so little now in anything or anyone that they would find it hard to understand the simplicity and intensity of faith with which these phrases were once taken among our troops, or the certitude felt by hundreds of thousands of men who are now dead that if they were killed their monument would be a new Europe not soured or soiled with the hates and greeds of the old. So we had failed - had won the fight and lost the prize; the garland of war was withered before it was gained. The lost years, the broken youth, the dead friends, the women's overshadowed lives at home, the agony and bloody sweat - all had gone to darken the stains which most of us had thought to scour out of the world that our children would live in. Many men felt, and said to each other, that they had been fooled."

For Montague the war had been corrosive on his ideals, his faith and his time away from his young family. But it had given him much to write about both for the paper and also for his books which he now hoped to also spend more time working on. Among those to flow from his pen are the novels A Hind Let Loose and Rough Justice as well as collections of short stories, other essays and a travel book.

He finally retired in 1925, and settled down to become a full-time writer in the last years of his life.

C. E. Montague died in Manchester on May 28th, 1928 at the age of 61.

Today Montague is seen as an Edwardian writer who, in his best work, was able to deliver the reality of the situations with their corrosive emotions and doubts. Though undervalued, much of his work has now begun to be again recognised for its honesty and its literary value. A writer with a sharp eye and keen ear and a brain unafraid to think things through and give us the benefit of those thoughts.

His collected papers are archived at John Rylands University.

Montague also wrote some poetry. Much of the conflict between his Christian faith and his soldierly duties are summed up in this poem:-

Unnamed Lines

Yes, of course it was sin
And no Christ would say `Fight
For the right' -
But we had to win.

When the chaplain would bluster and blow
About laying the rod
Of God
On the back of `His foe',

I knew it was all just a form,
And there was no fiery sword,
And the Lord
Was not in the storm.

Yet - to have stood aside
Hoarding my fortunate life
With my wife
While other men died!

Some sort of god, good or bad,
Would have kept me longing in vain
To be slain
As I am, if I had.

Written sometime in 1917

C. E. Montague – A Concise Bibliography

Dramatic Values (1911) Reviews
The Morning's War (1913) Novel
Disenchantment (1922) Essays on the First World War]
Fiery Particles (1923) Short stories (Another Temple Gone/Honours Easy/My Friend the Swan/A propos des Bottes/The First Blood Sweep/In Hanging Garden Gully/All for Peace and Quiet/Two or Three Witnesses/A Trade Report Only
A Hind Let Loose (1924) Novel
The Right Place (1924) Travel writing
Rough Justice (1926) Novel
Right off the Map (1927) Science fiction novel
Action (1928) Short stories (Action/A Cock and Bull Story/Sleep, Gentle Sleep/Judith/In the Ways of his Heart/A Pretty Little Property/The Great Sculling Race/Wodjabet/A Fatalist/Man Afraid/Ted's Leave/The Wisdom of Mrs. Trevanna/Didn't take Care of Himself
A Writer's Notes on His Trade (1930)

www.ingramcontent.com/pod-product-compliance
Lightning Source LLC
Chambersburg PA
CBHW071414170626
46811CB00003B/1399